Thanks to

those friends and readers who offered suggestions and encouragement:
**Gerald Dickinson, George Gibson, Judith Hodgson,
Tom Johnston** and **Jim Railton.**

Brian Cotton for his evocative front cover photograph.

Claire Bagness for her drawings of maps.

John Ferguson, author and compiler of Flodden data,
for his advice and interest.

Bill Grisdale for his valued effort,
for his imaginative and creative design of the book,
and for proposing its title.

David White, editor, whose ambition for accuracy and quality
never wavered, and whose vision of the novel extended my efforts
throughout its writing.

Dedicated to my mother
Hannah (Mallen) Hodgson
1914 - 2010

Introduction

The Battle of Flodden, 9th September 1513, fought by the armies of England and Scotland, has been portrayed as a significant turning point in the history of both nations. Essentially, it was a disastrous day for Scotland, and arguably, the nature of its defeat far exceeds the notion of an English victory.

The reasons behind the Scottish invasion and defeat lay culpably at the feet of the King of Scotland, James IV. A successful king during his reign, his death at Flodden and the grief caused by his failure not only overshadows his achievements as a celebrated monarch but also completely punctured the spirit and soul of his country and its people. Psychologically, the wound of the defeat seems as if it has never quite healed and a sense of remorse and sorrow lingers, even today, bound into the very name itself – Flodden.

Conceivably, part of a sense of shame later felt by the Scots may have lain in the fact that the English fighting at Flodden were from the northern counties and considered a mere second – and inferior – army to that which King Henry VIII had taken to France. Although this may well have been so, I can't imagine any other English force coping as strenuously as the Earl of Surrey's men did to gain an unlikely victory over a larger, more powerful Scottish army.

In 1976, visiting again the little village church at Branxton, I purchased a small booklet outlining the course of the battle, written by Jane Lyell and which is still available there, today. The brief, precise account was stimulating and furthered in me a fascination that has endured and resulted in numerous poems, as well as this latest work of fiction.

I say fiction, though the backbone of the story is by necessity factual. However, my intentions were straightforward: to tell the story of Flodden in an interesting, creative way, enlarging the plot and action with imaginative possibility. To this aim, I'm reminded of a line in Walter

Battle of Flodden 1513

Heron's Flight

Noel Hodgson

A NOVEL BY

Noel Hodgson

£4

The Reiver Press
The Old School House
Tillmouth
Cornhill-on-Tweed
TD12 4UT

First published in Great Britain by The Reiver Press, 2013

www.noelhodgson.co.uk

A CIP catalogue record for this book is available from the British Library.

ISBN 978-0-9545181-3-4

Printed and bound in Great Britain by The Billingham Press

Scott's famous poem, 'Marmion': *To tell red Flodden's dismal tale*

Recent books on the history of the battle, rather than other, older, romanticised accounts, proved valuable in gleaning further information that I could shape within my own work. These are: *Flodden 1513* by Niall Barr; *Flodden: A Scottish Tragedy* by Peter Reese; *From Boroughmuir To Branxton* by James Douglas Bell; and latterly, *The Battle Of Flodden – Why & How* by Clive Hallam-Baker. I recommend all four.

Not strictly bound by fact, I was able to dramatise and flesh out events with a sense of wonder and without fear of contradiction. In and around the course of action there would have been all sorts of goings-on… intrigue, incidents, disputes, rumours, cruelties and suchlike that added colour to the situation before, during and after the conflict. These scenes, though unrecorded, would surely have occurred though not, perhaps, as I have drawn them here.

The main characters involved in the conflict of 1513 are rightfully the leading players in my novel. Hopefully, their roles are revealed here as dynamic and credible.

King James of Scotland, in truth an efficient, popular king, was driven by illusions of grandeur and destiny. His ambition and sense of valour stoked a craving within him for military prowess that, in the end, proved his undoing. The English leader, the Earl of Surrey, wounded at the battle of Bosworth in 1485 and then imprisoned, was a remarkable survivor, and rose again in the realm. His wisdom and experience was key to victory. Surrey's son, Thomas Howard, the Lord Admiral, inherited similar qualities of leadership and his resolve was crucial. I have also chosen 'Bastard' Heron as a pivotal figure. As a fugitive from the law, his image, for me, has always seemed enigmatic – and it seemed right to inflate him into some kind of hero, albeit imperfect.

The Battle of Flodden in Northumberland was a major historical event: appalling, heroic and tragic – a battle worthy of respect and tribute, as the monument on Piper's Hill salutes. I trust that *Heron's Flight: Battle of Flodden, 1513*, may be read with this in mind, enlivening the deeds surrounding that murderous day.

Historical Summary

She was not beautiful but she was young. For a girl of fourteen years, Princess Margaret's skin was fresh, her face was clear eyed and in a plain way, attractive. As a diplomatic coup, her father, King Henry VII of England, strongly advocated her marriage to King James IV of Scotland. On her long journey north, grandly escorted through villages and towns, people lined the roads in celebration. The glorious wedding took place in Edinburgh, 1503. King James, handsome in all his splendour, was twice her age. It was, by all accounts, a suitably extravagant, lavish affair.

Previously, relations between the two countries had been strained for many years. In 1496, King James's attack on Norham Castle in his futile support of Perkin Warbeck's claim to the English Crown, followed by a larger incursion the year after, laying waste to several strongholds south of the River Tweed, underlined the tension that King Henry VII was eager to reconcile.

A truce at Ayton in 1497, followed by the 'Treaty of Perpetual Peace', negotiated and signed in 1502, led the way to a marriage which was, to all extent, an ideal arrangement, confirming both realms to a respectful and friendly relationship. Indeed, this settlement suited both kings. Relieved of the animosity that had marred their past, it allowed them to focus on stabilising their respective countries, overcoming any internal opposition to their power and authority. And so with optimism, it promised an era of security and progress.

Naturally, King James IV of Scotland, in the prime of life, overflowing with energy and self-confidence, saw it as a chance to further his ambitions. He was determined to extend and prosper his country's status, developing its economy and military capabilities on land and sea; a development that was encouraged by the French, but which England, lying between both nations, viewed with growing suspicion.

However, despite the 'Treaty of Perpetual Peace' and the 'marriage of appeasement', the Border region between England and Scotland still remained a wild, rugged, crime-ridden area. Raiding (known as reiving) and skirmishing continued, flouting laws that were difficult to enforce. The one-hundred-and-ten-miles-long Border, from sea to sea, was divided into three 'Marches' for governance: the West, the Middle and the East. Each section was policed by soldiers under the regulation of Wardens, an English and Scottish Warden for each March. Now and then, meetings between these authorities were arranged to deal with each side's complaints and grievances, but the unruly and scheming nature of the scattered Border population proved difficult to manage, with family allegiances and reprisals rife.

At one Wardens' meeting in 1508, the Scottish Middle March Warden, Sir Robert Ker, was murdered by the notorious English Border reiver 'Bastard' Heron and two associates, which greatly antagonised the Scots. This troublesome region, as well as King James's military ambitions supported by France, only aggravated the fragile, unhappy peace that was gradually eroding between the two neighbouring kingdoms.

After Henry VII died and his seventeen-year-old son, Henry VIII, was crowned in 1509, the belligerence of the young, arrogant English king imperilled the relationship further. Acts of confrontation increased around the Borderlands, and Henry's shameless withholding of his sister's inheritance infuriated King James. At sea, two important Scottish ships were captured by the English Navy, claiming that they were pirates, and prompting threats of retaliation. Finally, when learning of King Henry's plans to fight against France, the Scottish king, honour-bound, alerted his brother-in-law to Scotland's existing agreement with France – the 'Old Alliance', warning him of military intervention. King Henry had no intention of changing his mind and blatantly dismissed James's threats. As a result, in June 1513, with Henry's army sailing off to fight in France, the eleven-year-old 'Treaty of Perpetual Peace' was doomed.

In early August that same year, a Scottish raiding army of some seven thousand men under Alexander, Lord Home, caused grief and harassment throughout Northumberland. On their return journey, however, Sir William Bulmer, acting Warden of England's East March, with his one thousand archers ambushed their booty-laden train near Milfield, inflicting an ignominious defeat. Despite this ominous event, known as the 'Ill Raid', it was King James and his army's invasion into England, on 22nd August, that saw the said treaty finally and irrevocably broken. And as history shows, the savage war ended drastically for King James IV and Scotland, at the Battle of Flodden on 9th September 1513.

Throughout the years preceding the battle, involved directly or indirectly in practically every major dealing between the two countries, one significant English figure remained prominent: none other than Thomas Howard, the Earl of Surrey and General of the North, who led his troops to victory in that ultimate, bloody conflict.

The English and Scottish Armies

Senior English Commanders
under the leadership of Thomas Howard, Earl of Surrey.
Thomas Howard, Lord Admiral
Edmund Howard
Sir Marmaduke Constable
Lord Thomas Dacre
Sir Edward Stanley
Sir William Bulmer

Senior Scottish Commanders
under the leadership of King James IV of Scotland.
Alexander, Lord Home
Alexander Gordon, Earl of Huntly
John Lindsay, Earl of Crawford
William Hay, Earl of Errol
William Graham, Earl of Montrose
Adam Hepburn, Earl of Bothwell
Matthew Stewart, Earl of Lennox
Archibald Campbell, Earl of Argyll

HERON'S FLIGHT
Battle of Flodden 1513

Below Dover Castle, the bay was abustle with flapping sails. A war fleet, its galleys like a gathering flock of gulls, was being loaded with a cargo of equipment, provisions and soldiers. Noisy spectators thronged the shore. Banners and flags jostled in a lively breeze. From the tower's height, England's young, proud king and his company of noblemen surveyed the dazzling scene and its carnival-like atmosphere.

Soon to depart with his army for France, Henry VIII confronted Thomas Howard, Earl of Surrey. The king's eyes shone. Thrusting his hand upon the old earl's broad shoulder, he first reminded his audience of Scotland's counter-threat, to invade England. "I trust them not. Once my back is turned to contest the French, King James has sworn ruination of our Borderlands. I shall not give way. His mischief shall be met." He paused, aiming his words at Howard alone. "I and Queen Catherine have entrusted you, sire, to defend the realm against the Scots. I beseech you to prepare an army worthy of guarding and protecting our nation in my absence." His stance shifted, a slight alteration that effected a change of voice. "Let it be heard – I depend upon you, Surrey."

As he listened, Surrey felt the weight of Henry's hand upon him like a royal seal, setting grave importance to the king's words and to the responsibility he laid upon his noble commander.

Later, from time to time, on his way north from London, Thomas Howard recalled the zeal of King Henry's stare and heard, again and again, His Majesty's final sentence wheeling through his mind: "I depend upon you, Surrey!" It was the appeal in his tone – wedged by a faint desperation – more than the words themselves that inscribed them upon the earl's memory. Secretly, in a corner of Surrey's mind, he sometimes considered that the young king's brazen, public display was not entirely genuine.

****

Stopping briefly at his home in Norfolk to bid farewell to his family, the earl, now alone with his wife, held her in a firm embrace, kissed her cheek lightly and then gazed at her lovingly, his face close to hers. He smiled, eyes full of tenderness. Lady Agnes ran her fingers down his cheek, its skin drawn and mottled with age. Her lips pursed, restraining the fears that gnawed at her feelings. "I shall pray each day for your safe deliverance, and that of my two stepsons, Thomas and Edmund," she confided. A woman of thirty-five, half his age, she looked older than her years, small and poised, with an intense looking expression that drained her face of its beauty.

A cousin to his first wife, Elizabeth, who had died sixteen years earlier, they had later married and together had already increased his family with three more children plus another on the way. Sensitive to his mission, of his going off to war, leaving her and their young children behind, she clearly knew the risks he faced of failure, defeat and possible death, and found it difficult to hide her anxiety for his safety and survival.

Surrey squeezed her hand. "Agnes, my dear wife. I shall pray for you each day also, for your wellness and fortitude." He kissed her palm, signifying his devotion to her. "King Henry has bestowed upon me the honour of defending our country in the north while he leads his own army from the south, to fight in France." His look tightened as vehemence coated his next words. "Despite the taint of Wolsey upon it, I shall perform my duty with diligence and pride."

Thomas Howard, Earl of Surrey, and other senior advisers to the monarch, were pained to observe the favoured, manipulative Wolsey overtaking them as he gained greater influence in the king's court. Wolsey, of humble birth, had risen through the church to the position of Royal Chaplain and then, at the new, young king's directive, had been promoted to the higher post of Almoner, which permitted him a seat on the Privy Council.

Lady Howard gazed upon her husband with affection. "I do not doubt it, Thomas, but I dare to say, in the privacy of this room, that it is a young and rash king who would place this burden upon you."

The earl raised his eyebrows to check her complaint. "Some words are best unspoken," he admonished her, lightly. "But I assure you, Agnes, I am capable of the responsibility," he added teasingly, "and I know, my good Lady, not to fight as a young man." He paused, eyes sharpening, and his tone deepened. "Of course, I wish to please my king and although I would have preferred that I sail with him and his army to France, I cannot refuse his behest." Thomas Howard's voice softened yet he remained earnest. "However, more than any other wish, it is you, my beloved, that I shall endeavour to please. Whatever happens, I shall not disappoint you nor bring shame upon this house and family."

Lady Agnes regarded his rugged countenance and saw the striking face of an elderly man whose self-belief and integrity had never wavered, regardless of those accusations and criticisms that had penalised him in the past, culminating in the loss of his rightful dukedom.

At the Battle of Bosworth, 1485, the earl had fought on the side of the then king, Richard III. A victorious Henry Tudor had ordered Thomas Howard to be imprisoned in the Tower and removed of his powers and lands.

However, the newly crowned King Henry VII was not so inclined to execute a true and noble soldier of Howard's value. Assured by the earl's promise of loyalty to his country and king, Henry released Howard and reinstated his military and courtly duties though not his rightful ducal title, which was due him as a consequence of his father's death at Bosworth.

Agnes considered her husband's candid, heartfelt words and was aware of what they implied. She drew a long breath. "I understand, my lord. Forgive my heart's worry. It is selfish of me and unhelpful."

Surrey adored Agnes's strength of character. When his first wife died and he was torn by grief and despair, Agnes had provided him with solace, understanding and companionship. Their friendship, despite their difference in years, had developed naturally and his fondness for her had grown and deepened with genuine warmth and passion. He gazed at her, his eyes glistening. "I worry also for my country and its safety," he admitted. "But, beyond my duty, you must remember, dearest, that it is my love of you and our children that fires my being." Thomas Howard paused, straightening his shoulders and his bearing. "With God's Grace, I shall return," he asserted. He embraced her tenderly and, kissing her once more, he turned and moved stiffly towards the door that led into the great hall, where his retinue of senior household guards awaited him.

His men accompanied him outside and into the courtyard to his covered carriage, which stood ready. Helped into it, he sat down alone and, without a backward glance, set off to join his five hundred trained soldiers assembled in the grounds. Passing through the wide, open gates leading from his estate, the earl's train veered right to continue its journey north, to Pontefract Castle, already selected as his initial military headquarters.

2

Surrey's confidence and resolution were based on a life of service to the English Crown and a generalship that was much respected and admired. Indeed, he had more military experience than any other living Englishman and had proven to be a remarkable leader of men. His knowledge of the northern counties and his influence with its lords and barons was vital in assembling an army to face the Scots.

In a letter he had sent to his young wife, in early August, Surrey wrote confirming that preparations had been made throughout July, contacting and instructing his main commanders "to further organise and equip their forces of regular soldiers, and levies from the lands and townships under their governance." He went on to say, "It is of comfort and fitting that I know these noblemen well and trust them as friends." What his modesty would not permit him to add was that they, in turn, fully respected the redoubtable soldier he had proven himself to be.

Thomas Howard, the earl, had campaigned in Northumberland before; most notably, in response to King James's brief incursion into

England in 1496, adding might to Perkin Warbeck's futile claim to the English throne; and then again the following year when the Scottish king invaded in retaliation for English aggression at sea. Because of these and other engagements, Surrey was familiar with the Border country, with lowland Scotland and its volatile, determined leader. Regardless of King Henry VIII's primary concern, fighting in France with his elite commanders, gunners and troops to support him, there was no one more suited than the stately earl to deal with Scotland's latest, major threat of invasion.

On 25th August, as soon as news reached Pontefract that a huge Scottish army had crossed the Border a few days earlier and had begun destroying English strongholds along the River Tweed, Surrey swiftly alerted his allies so that they might muster at Newcastle. In a hasty message to Lady Agnes, he concluded, "God has now called upon me to fulfil the task that I was set. I fear it not. Through your continuing prayer, I strongly believe that I shall have faith and courage and love to withstand the challenges which lie ahead."

On his way north from Pontefract, stopping at York and then Durham, Surrey's own troops were joined by more and more recruits, expanding his army. Significantly, it was at Durham that the earl requested he borrow the banner of St Cuthbert. This was a wise decision, for the holy relic, a venerable beacon of triumph over adversity, symbolised faith and belief in the mission.

Arriving at Newcastle on 30th August, Surrey's army grew to over twenty-thousand men, including an artillery train that had arrived two days earlier from London. Stormy weather had made the journey north difficult. However, greeted and surrounded by his comrades, Sir Marmaduke Constable from Yorkshire, Sir William Bulmer from Durham, Lord Thomas Dacre from Cumbria and, soon after, by Lord Edward Stanley from Lancashire, Surrey's resolve and confidence were reignited by their faithful company and their assurance to serve under him.

These leaders understood, implicitly, that he would not regard or treat them as subordinates, and that he would make no decisions without their say. All were powerful, robust commanders in their own right, offering maturity, reliability and a commitment to his generalship. Having members of their own families accompanying them, they also accepted, unreservedly, the appointment of Surrey's sons – Thomas, the Lord Admiral, and the younger Edmund, to the English forces' hierarchy; such was their esteem for the Howard name, and its bold and righteous reputation.

At Newcastle, the organisation of Surrey's army was rapidly developed, with officers and sergeants being designated to specific units of men. Despite the dismaying absence of the earl's elder son, Lord Admiral Thomas Howard, delayed at sea by storms, the English army progressed through foul weather and mud-clogged roads to the castle at Alnwick. Halting briefly there, they were reinforced by the brothers William and Lionel Percy and their soldiers. The Percys' elder brother, Henry, the fifth Earl of Northumberland and Warden of the East March, had already departed Alnwick in June to fight alongside King Henry VIII in France.

Having rested outside the town's walls and taken on much needed supplies, the English army under Surrey was about to move on towards the village of Bolton, twelve miles south of Wooler, when the Lord Admiral finally arrived. The old earl was overjoyed, embracing his son. "We are relieved to welcome you and your men," he declared, surrounded by his leaders. Accompanying the admiral were one thousand highly trained mariners from the Fleet. The addition of these disciplined, professional fighting men was viewed with awe and admiration, for they appeared supreme. What's more, in the eyes of ordinary soldiers, they seemed invincible.

At the sprawling campsite beside Bolton, Monday 5th September, Surrey's army was fully gathered and ready to challenge the Scots. At a meeting with his war council, final decisions were made regarding the formation of the vanguard, to be led by the admiral, and that of the rearguard, to be controlled by the Earl of Surrey himself, overall Commander-in-Chief.

Strategically, Surrey and his council were fully reconciled and prepared to engage the Scottish army in battle. Their planning, however, was now hinged to the growing problem of holding on to their own weather-beaten army, which was rapidly running short of food and drink. Even Lord Stanley, a strict, ardent leader, was particularly concerned at the state of his own soldiers, impoverished by cold and damp which had blighted their nights' sleep since leaving home. He described it colourfully, without amusement. "Already, the rash of their reluctance is rising. Their eyes are heavy and movement slothful. In days to come their very jowls will scrape the ground."

Thus, desperate to commit the Scots to a fight as soon as possible, Surrey promptly sent his herald, Rouge Croix, to King James – residing at Ford Castle, formally challenging him to meet in battle on Milfield Plain no later than Friday 9th September. To provoke this action, Surrey's son, the admiral, in a separate note, added his own insults to rankle the king, boasting of his fleet's dominance at sea and the capture of two Scottish ships for alleged acts of piracy.

"I cannot see a leader as pompous as King James refusing our offer to fight," remarked Edmund Howard later, in the private company of his father and older brother.

"It is not a question of fighting," replied the admiral, irritably. "Fight they must. But for our sake it cannot be delayed. Our father has already made that clear." He sniffed and then sighed loudly, displaying his ill humour.

Edmund glanced at his father, seated opposite him, and smiled in deference. "Of course. But there are rumours that the Scots have no real cause to fight, their king's invasion being a mere show, a curtsy to France and its lovely queen."

Surrey returned the smile. Too often Edmund's flippant remarks were aimed at irking his severe-minded older brother. "Rumours make no difference to the fact that King James leads a great army and waits with it on English soil," his father answered with composure. "But now that he has been challenged, we can do no more than await his reply."

Though fraught with anticipation, Surrey could not allow his two sons to perceive how anxious he was to hear of King James's response. Under-rationed, weary of marching, and depressed by storms of wind and rain, the morale of his men was bound to decline further in the coming days. He had seen it before, in other conflicts – the sway of troops whose willingness to fight had shrivelled quickly, plagued by hunger, misery and poor health. He determined with all his power that they would meet the Scottish enemy before it was too late, for it was glaringly clear to him that his time was limited.

3

Unlike the English soldiers, the Scots were more adequately provided. A direct line of supplies from Edinburgh, some sixty miles away to the north, reached down through Coldstream to replenish their stocks. Nevertheless, having already ravaged and pillaged a wide area of the countryside surrounding their encampment on Flodden Hill, greedy bands of looters continued to wander further afield in search of bounty.

"Look, yonder," one of the horsemen urged, pointing. The band of Scottish robbers, with their loaded wagon and trailing livestock, pulled up. Through the drizzle they spied a thin feather of smoke rising above the trees below. Carefully, they steered their horses down off the crag near Hazelrigg and, leaving the wagon guarded by four footmen, the main group of thirteen horsemen followed a muddy track into the wood, leading to a clearing where a huddle of shabby wooden buildings crouched in shelter. Apart from the smoking chimney there seemed to be no other sign of life.

"Aa dinna' like it," muttered one of the bedraggled bunch, sensing danger. They stopped, expressions creased with uncertainty as they turned their heads, staring round.

From the dark, dank undergrowth a flock of arrows swished through the air. Five of the Scotsmen gasped and toppled from their mounts while the other eight wheeled round, swords and spears raised. Charging out from hiding, thirty enemy horsemen wearing red neckerchiefs swarmed towards them, circling the unfortunates. In a short, noisy melee with bawls and screams ripping the air, the outnumbered Scots were mercilessly hacked down, none escaping or spared.

Hearing the clamour, the four left behind with the booty ran into the wood to escape. The dumb cluster of pigs and two cows standing motionless beside the loaded wagon raised their heads as six other horsemen galloped past in pursuit of the fugitives. Out of sight in the trees, a commotion of resounding yells and shouts abruptly ceased, ending the affair.

When the three-dozen English horsemen gathered, a single prisoner, roped at the neck, was yanked forward by a large rider. Fearing his punishment, the Scot whimpered in terror. The big man on the horse dismounted and shoved the prisoner towards his leader, seated astride a speckled roan stallion. "This'n put up his hands an' wouldn't fight," said the tall one, called Straughen, his mouth curling with disdain for the man's cowardliness.

The outlaw, John Heron, his eyes as black as his sleek, shoulder-length hair, scowled down at the wretch and, using the tip of his blooded sword, he lifted the man's bearded chin to view his face. "Go back to your countrymen and warn them of this," he rasped. "Let them know that we're here, everywhere, watching, night and day." His speech was measured, with barely a trace of accent, clearly an educated man.

Realising that he was allowed to live, the prisoner's mouth opened with relief and his eyes brightened. He nodded, his tongue sliding back and forth across his hairy, lower lip as he sneaked a faint, leering look of pleasure at the imposing horseman, unmistakable in his red cape.

'Bastard' Heron stared down, perceiving the man's lurid expression, and intuitively saw the sneer of a brute; the kind of bully he recalled tormenting him in childhood for being what he was; an outsider and unwanted. Sullenly, he remembered the pain of those boys' taunts, and worse, the blows of rejection. He looked hard into the burly man's face and he recognised the spitefulness and meanness of a thug. And without a word or hint of a change of mind, he rammed his blade into the man's throat. The robber's face blanked then grimaced in shock and agony before his body slithered to the ground, jerking and kicking.

The other riders did not move or speak. They'd witnessed Heron's sinister, cruel streak before, and its ruthlessness. But they were hardened reiver men and he was their champion. Thus, with respect, not apprehension, they awaited his next command.

"Weatherburn," instructed Heron, "you and Joe Telfer, and Thompson and Hedley take care of the cart and animals. Straughen, get the four Dunne brothers and some others to assist you and see to the dead bodies. Strip them of weapons and anything else you want of value, and tie two together at a time onto the poorest of their horses, then drive them over the river towards the Scottish camp on Flodden. I want it to be shown, as a threat, what will happen to other scavengers. We'll keep the best horses for ourselves."

Heron stooped and wiped his sword's blade clean on the dead man's sleeve. He thrust the sword back into its sheath looped to his saddle. "We'll meet up later before dark in the wood above the waterfall at Roughting Linn," he ended, looking round at his outlaw troop. Since none of his henchmen had anything to add, he turned his horse, and with Hinson, his second in command, riding alongside him, he led the rest of his gang away, up the crag and onto the bleak, misty moor.

4

Monday evening. Within the walls of Ford Castle, which the Scots had commandeered, Lady Elizabeth Heron sat demurely at the large dining table, opposite King James. During their meal, with other Scottish nobles present – Huntly, Crawford, Errol, Montrose and Bothwell, they had exchanged few words, the king's moroseness casting ill-ease amongst them. Now that they had finished eating, he demanded that she alone should accompany him to the adjacent room, to sit by the fireside. The others stood up to bow as their king and the Lady Heron departed, and remained on their feet until a servant had closed the door behind the pair.

In the private room, King James politely indicated for her to sit beside him on the velvet-cushioned chair angled towards the arching fireplace, where logs burned brightly. She obeyed and he took her hand at once and kissed it, while peering strangely at her face and the pale, serene beauty of its fine features, as if for the first time. Her lips moved as though she were about to speak. He raised a finger and placed it over her mouth, to stem her words.

"We shall be leaving this place come morning. Surrey's army at Bolton will head north tomorrow, to set up camp beside Wooler in readiness for battle. It is my duty to be with my army now, day and night." His voice sounded thin, as though he were uttering another's lines.

But to Lady Heron's ears, he spoke with resignation and in an odd manner that appeared indifferent to her being in the room and to any relationship between them. Turning his head, he stared absently into the fire's flames, fingering the large turquoise ring that the French queen had sent him as a gift, accompanying her request that he aid her country by opposing England with force. Lady Heron sensed with trepidation the change in him but knew better than to reply straight away. Again, with great formality he took her hand in his. "We thank you, Lady Elizabeth, for your accommodation and," he paused, his tone edged by a certain coolness, "for your hospitality."

Slowly, he raised his hand again and gripped her shoulder. She considered his hold careless, even rough. Slighted by his harsh manner and words, her breath deepened with a sense of indignation. "My husband William lies imprisoned, at your mercy. It behoves me to do what I can, for both him and you."

King James stared at her, already his for the taking, and frowned, resentful of what she insinuated. Letting his hand bearing the ring slide down, brushing her breast, he smiled sourly. "When we return to Edinburgh I shall order his release and let him favour my Queen in return for your service."

Lady Heron withdrew herself, sitting back, stung by the impropriety of his insult. "Forgive me, Your Majesty, but that remark is unbecoming of a king whose presence and affection I have accepted with an open, caring heart."

He forced a slight, sardonic laugh and heaved a long breath, as if to inflate his spleen. "We have brought a great army into England. It is well armed, trained and powerful. We shall defeat old Surrey and your country will shudder enough to halt young King Henry's ambitions in France. Of course you care, Lady Elizabeth. You have no choice. You and your husband kneel at my mercy." His jaw tightened, holding the emotion stifled beneath his proud, determined aspect. Since his arrival he had been courteous and gentle towards her. Now he spoke with reproach, even disdain.

Lady Heron regarded him in silence. Was this, she considered, his way of asserting himself above the doubts that surrounded his reason to invade, and which cramped his authority. He had proven an able king, uniting his country, developing its wealth, strength, and status. And now for the sake of France, and the personal request of its artful queen that he honour the Old Alliance between their countries, he'd stepped into England with an army, more, it seemed, as a gesture of compliance and self-esteem, than with any real intent to advance further south to conquer and inflict greater damage.

During his stay here at Ford Castle, Lady Heron's attention and intimacy had invoked his confidence, his tenderness and desire. But now, confronted by an event riskier than any other in his life, it seemed he needed to dismiss her, a woman, coveting, he suspected, more of his charity than of himself. She knew in his nightly caresses and kisses that he craved her affection, but here now was a different man; an insensitive, vindictive king, stubborn, arrogant, and fixed to a role that wilfully repelled any hint of frailty.

In the silence that separated them, he had released her hand and, his expression tense, watched again the flames that twisted and curled above the burning logs. Turning curtly to meet her eyes, he stroked the ring as he spoke. "I shall not see you this night and I leave at dawn. I have ordered the castle to be destroyed ere midday. Make ready to depart in safety," James advised, flatly, then promptly stood. "In time I shall return to find you," he added, blandly. The Lady Elizabeth did not reply. He raised his hand so that she might kiss it. Meekly, she obliged, and then watched him stride out of the room.

Alone, confounded, she herself now gazed into the fire, her pulse racing, her thoughts darting, her breathing quick and short. Shaken by her humiliation, her bruised heart pounded.

5

Awakened by the sounds of horses, Lady Elizabeth Heron slipped from her bed and, wrapping a shawl about her, tiptoed to the window to peer out into the mauve light of early dawn. Beyond the River Till, across the vale, she spied the stoked fires of the Scottish camp on Flodden Hill. Her gaze fell into the courtyard where King James and his nobles and household guards were gathering to leave. She knew she could not be seen yet her heart fluttered with a slim hope that he might pause and glance up towards her room, affording her some attention, some value. She waited in vain for they moved away, dark riders, towards the outer gate, disappearing into the leafy avenue of trees leading down to the river. She rested her head against a shutter, her feelings perplexed and drained by all that she had endured these past days.

In her lingering, Lady Elizabeth heard a sound across the dimly lit room. She froze. The door opened and then closed. "Who is it?" she called in alarm. She recognised his voice as he answered with his name, approaching her. She braced herself. John Heron stood before her, his solemn, handsome face glowing in the pale light of the window. "How dare you enter my chamber," she exclaimed.

"I may not be a king, but now he's gone from here, surely a Heron deserves a modest, genteel greeting?" he answered cynically.

She winced. She knew her companionship with King James would be a cause for local gossip and her reputation sullied, but for him, John Heron, to allude to it was offensive, and her mind throbbed with exasperation. After all, it was his part in the murder of the Scottish Warden, Sir Robert Ker, and his subsequent flight from justice that had resulted in her husband's imprisonment in Fast Castle, east of Edinburgh – hostage for a crime that he had not committed.

"Is it beyond your imagination to see it was for William's release that I was prepared to be the king's hostess, to give of myself? A predicament,

I remind you, caused solely by your doing." She glared, her chestnut-coloured eyes wide, smouldering with fury. "If there is shame in it, then be it yours too, John Heron."

He gave her a quizzical look. "Oh yes, yes, I have shame enough, and pain. You were my first and only love, but it was denied by your father, and mine who preferred your marriage to his favoured and rightful son, my half-brother." He paused, his jaw tight for a moment as he checked his emotion. "But let us not talk of it again, such disappointment and betrayal, Lady Elizabeth, when present matters weigh so much more heavily upon us." He subdued his own bitterness in order to continue temperately. "What news have you that the English army may depend on?"

Her temper calmed. She moved past him, and away from the window, to the side of her bed. He followed, but she remained standing and with her back to him. "Surrey's army is due to reach Wooler this very day, Tuesday. Late yesterday, letters were exchanged and the battle has been set for no later than noon, this coming Friday, 9th September. As you doubtless know already, King James left here but recently to join his troops," she stated tersely, separating each piece of information with precision. She paused. "Despite some desertion, his army numbers well over thirty-thousand soldiers. However, I believe a few of the Scottish nobles remain silently opposed to the invasion and to their king's headstrong leadership. His mind is afflicted by his duty to his nation, his vision, and the expectation he places upon himself." She drew breath to continue. "Sometime this morning, Ford Castle is due to be destroyed under orders from King James himself. He asked me to choose between the life of my husband or the castle," she ended on a lowering note.

John Heron made no reply and his silence lengthened until she turned to face him. "What are your thoughts? What can be done?" she asked earnestly.

"He will die for it. And for the abuse of you. I give you my word," he said coldly. She stared nervously at the enmity in his eyes; a look, she recalled, that had always inhibited her affection towards him. She remembered, especially, the malicious streak within him that alarmed her and others. Once, when a group of them, no more than ten years old, still young and playful, were idling down by the river, he attacked a cousin of hers who had teased him, punching his victim repeatedly until other boys were forced to drag him off. It was this ferocity, and the venom in it, which she now perceived again in his look and reply, that had eventually scared her away from him and his ardour.

As ever, dazzled by her loveliness, Heron felt the sudden temptation to draw her into his arms, to protect and save her, but knew that she would resist him, repelling his desire. He gazed into her dark, brown eyes then bowed his head in courteous farewell, turned about and furtively slipped from the room as he had entered, like a thief.

Lady Heron sat down wearily on the edge of the bed and as tears filled her eyes she lay on her back, closing them, her lips nipped tight with exhaustion and torment. Though she dreaded the ruination of her home, she feared more the approaching days and the crisis facing them all. And then, beyond reason, against all sense, she desperately wished that before he'd left, he'd returned to embrace and kiss her once more.

6

Tuesday noontime on Flodden Hill. Grim-faced, King James read the latest messages recently delivered from the English camp at Wooler. The first of these came from Surrey; the second, scornful threats again from the earl's son, Admiral Howard. In effect, they desired the Scottish army to come down off the hill to fight a battle that would be fair to both sides. In their appeal they made it explicit that it was only gallant to do so, thereby challenging the king's sense of chivalry. In a separate note, the admiral threatened him that if he refused to comply there would be no mercy shown – no lives spared, no prisoners taken. James suppressed his anger at this ultimatum so that none present would see his reaction, especially Surrey's weasel-eyed herald, Rouge Croix, who stood flanked by guards, awaiting the king's reply. Without speaking, James signalled the guards to remove the English herald, by name Thomas Hawley, from the royal pavilion. Before turning, the squat-looking Hawley bowed insipidly, resigned to his inevitable detention, a customary ploy before battle in order to delay information passing to the enemy.

Once Rouge Croix had been escorted from the room, James handed both letters to his main commanders: Lord Home, with the earls – Huntly, Crawford, Errol, Bothwell, Montrose, Lennox and Argyll who were seated in a semi-circle, anticipating his response. As each in turn read the missives and passed them on, the king began to rant.

"How dare that mere earl, too ancient and crippled even to ride a horse, question my right, a king, to deploy my troops how and where I choose?" His face reddened. "The time and day of the conflict has been settled. We shall not move from this hill for the sake of his convenience, nor in consequence of the threats made against us by his insolent son. Our guns are set in place, our soldiers are well instructed and our pike columns, trained by our French allies, are ready to devastate the English. Everything is organised to our advantage. If they cannot match us then let Surrey bear his failure, and its disgrace, on his flight south!"

Adam Hepburn, the second Earl of Bothwell and close friend to James, nodded in accord. "Well said, Your Majesty. But perhaps it is worth reminding ourselves how crafty and wily Surrey can be. We can guarantee that he will fight, though he is clearly cautious of the strength of our position. I agree with you, my king, that we should not move, but I urge us to beware."

The others were of the same mind and James was pleased with their support. There had been some dissent from the very start of the campaign, with particular criticism of French influence and their involvement, and it had aggravated him. Now the engagement was near, he felt morale growing, empowering him.

"I thank you each for your countenance. I will reply with good haste," he concluded, standing up with an assured flourish to signal an end to the meeting.

Unusually, his commanders remained sitting, contrary to protocol. James sensed their need to speak with him further. Willingly, he sat down again and bade them speak. It was John Lindsay, Earl of Crawford, who stirred from his seat. He bowed judiciously towards his king. "Sire," he commenced, his manner endearing, "we admire our king for the good he has done and the achievements of his reign. Indeed, through your zeal and vision Scotland has thrived and risen as never before. We are thus indebted to your purpose, your energy and endeavour. Yet here, now, we are faced with a conflict exceeding any previous encounter on English soil. We in this room do not doubt its validity and your authority. We know that you will fight fiercely and skilfully, more so than any other man." Lindsay leaned forward, bringing his fingertips together.

"Your courage, honour, determination and desire for victory is inspiring. Yet, my good king, we are sorely troubled. You wish to lead us into battle, to front the assault, as a great and bold leader. Alas, Your Majesty, a great leader does not always prove to be a great general. At the head of your army you will be either casualty or hero. Your loss, Heaven forbid, would prove catastrophic to the morale of our troops. Therefore, noble king, we plead that you govern the day's victory by overseeing it from a safer, more advantageous position, directing your army accordingly."

King James rose from his seat. Vexation flushed his cheeks though his words were constrained. "What I ask of any soldier I ask of myself." He bristled. "With or without me, victory shall be ours. I demand that you leave the decision in my hands and have faith in what I desire. I have no cause to doubt any of you and I expect this trust to be returned in full. My intent shall not alter. Let this be enough of it," he ended, curtly, and with a flick of his hand, indicated for them to exit the room immediately.

In silence, one by one, each commander rose, bowed and departed from him. Only the Earl of Bothwell, last to go, hesitated. James eyed him firmly. "If you wish to add to what Lindsay has said then I'll have none of it," he admonished.

Bothwell replied that he had other news, informing his king that Ford

Castle had been set afire earlier in the morning, though the Bastard Heron and his followers, in an attempt to thwart the destruction, had ambushed a small company of Scottish soldiers as they forded the river, killing and wounding a number. "By the time help had arrived, Your Majesty, the attackers had taken off, fleeing into the woods towards higher ground. I regret that Heron has evaded capture once again," despaired the earl.

Lightly tugging the turquoise ring on his finger, King James pondered the news. He looked past Bothwell. "Pray tell me," he enquired, "what of Lady Heron and her safety?"

"I can assure you, most noble king, that Lady Heron departed the castle in good time, before its destruction. Escorted by a troop of my soldiers for most of the way, her transport then continued to Berwick, which remains in English hands." Bothwell gave a reverential nod. "Sire, I have been informed that Lady Heron safely entered the town, and has already joined her daughter who found refuge there prior to our advance into England."

King James continued to stare absently; unresponsive to the answer he had sought from the earl.

Bothwell hesitated. Alarmingly, he had seen the change in James. The invasion seemed to have become his dream – the battle signifying more than simply an opportunity to prove his nation's might. It was to be his theatre, and him to play the major part, the glittering role of the hero king that he'd always wished to fulfil. His desperation for it was acute, afflicting his very nature. Bothwell felt the weight of a dark cloud upon him. He could smell violence, like thunder, and it unnerved him.

To close the meeting, King James suddenly regarded the earl, acknowledging him. "You, Adam Hepburn, more than any other here, understand me. My duty as a king is foremost in my mind. I cannot allow my purpose to weaken. If I am wrong, tell me as a good friend and a true subject."

Bothwell smiled faintly, unable at this moment to express his inner fears. "You are not wrong. You are an eminent king and we shall stand with you," he answered carefully. He knew the strain King James was under and how isolated he'd become. He would have liked to say more on the matter of his generalship, but for now, it was enough to console him.

James smiled, showing his gratitude, and after Bothwell had gone, a servant brought James parchment, pen and ink to compose his reply to Surrey. Writing furiously, aiming to belittle the English commander and his foolish entreaty, the king tersely scorned the English resolve to fight and stated bluntly that the Scottish army would not descend the hill to do battle, but hold the high ground at his own pleasure and not be persuaded otherwise by inferior persons.

Meanwhile, outside the pavilion, the lively Scottish herald, Lord Islay, waited on horseback, ready to deliver the king's missive at speed to the English, encamped at Wooler.

7

On the flat land known as the Haugh, on the east side of the small river flowing below the abandoned settlement of Wooler, the English army had settled into its latest camp. The soldiers were resting from the weariness and misery of their march north, having endured for a week or more the seemingly endless gusts of rain and wind.

Listless and morose, the men's morale was visibly weakening. Not only was the bad weather inflicting illness on many but also food rations were so meagre that they were being underfed. The Scots had previously scavenged the region leaving it bare and, to make matters worse, supply wagons sent from Newcastle, intended to ease the situation, had been stolen on the way by local robbers. For the Earl of Surrey and his commanders, consternation was growing, clawing at their minds.

Since an explanation was justifiable to all those prepared to sacrifice themselves, stories surrounding the conflict and its cause were repeated throughout the lower ranks. In order to motivate groups of levy soldiers, sergeants were instructed to tell them of King Henry's invasion of France and how Scotland, on the side of the French, had gathered a vast army in Edinburgh and then crossed into England.

"To oppose their aggression," one sergeant declared, "our king ordered the Earl of Surrey to muster an English army to repel the Scots, and shame their king, James IV." The sergeant made clear that despite the earl being a man of seventy years, lamed by action, wear and age, he was nevertheless a shrewd and powerful general. "A true leader," the man vouched, "capable of rallying his army to defend and save England from the invading Scots." To further allay his listeners' mute concern, the sergeant described the frailty of many in the Scottish army as poor, useless pitchfork fighters. "And I tell you, fellow soldiers, that there're hundreds of half-brained vagrants and ragamuffins amongst them that'll run off at the first sight of danger," he scorned.

A little later, huddled around a damp, sizzling wood fire, a Yorkshireman named Richard turned to his friend. "Now William, me heard the same thing was telt t' other groups o' men about the Scottish peasants. Them bein' useless an' a' that. Those louse-bitten sergeants must've all been telt t' say the same," he sneered.

William pulled a face. "Does them think we're daft? A'd say a pitchfork up the arse in't useless. A'd say nowt's worse, lad," he argued, scratching his stubbly chin.

Amused by his friend's drollness, Richard's shoulders trembled as he stifled a chuckle.

****

Unlike King James who stood alone, even aloof, from his war council, Surrey had his two sons, Thomas, Lord Admiral, and the younger Edmund alongside him, both loyal to the core. He also counted on the mutual and faithful respect of his other main commanders, Lord Thomas Dacre, Sir Edward Stanley, Sir Marmaduke Constable and Sir William Bulmer.

The condition of their troops prior to going into battle was worrisome, yet the overriding challenge lay in the Scottish position, solidly entrenched on Flodden Hill. Furthermore, the wiry Scottish herald, Islay, had, earlier that afternoon, delivered the king's riposte: that he refused to move from the hill. Surrey and his leaders were in no doubt; to engage the Scottish army in battle from the plain below would surely prove fatal. Painfully, the old earl's predicament held him by the throat. He was honour-bound by the rules of engagement to fight the Scottish army in three days time: Friday 9th September. To delay would seem an admission of surrender and would allow James to lead his army back into Scotland, heads held high, his mission achieved. Thomas Howard knew such an outcome would brand himself as a failed leader, his power as a general blemished and his standing no longer credited within England.

In a large, ransacked house on the southern edge of the camp, Surrey, his sons and other commanders were seated around a table, debating alternative tactics to the planned confrontation at Flodden that they believed to be unfair and ruinous to them. The tension revealed itself in the silence that followed each proposition, indicating either reluctance or a rejection of it. If fight they must, the only approach that would seem to give the English army an even chance would be from the north, between Flodden and Branxton Hill, in sight of the River Tweed.

But how to reach Branxton Hill, beyond the range of the Scottish guns, would surely prove both strenuous and hazardous. There was, as well, the risk of arriving too late, with the Scottish army by then retreating back into Scotland. Surrey sensed the others' frustration. He sat upright in his chair, drawing attention.

"Let us put it aside for now. Go to your duties, speak with your captains and we shall meet again in two hours. I assure you, a decision must be made. Time is against us but we shall not be rash. We will not throw ourselves into a lions' den without hope. My years tell me that valour and folly are no further apart than the thickness of a sword's blade." He snorted, and shrugged lightly. "Go now. I need to rest and think on it. Perhaps in a dream an answer might be found," he said, looking over them all with a faint smile on his lips. Glancing at his sons, he asked of them that they pray alongside him before they too departed.

While the two brothers remained, the other four leaders smiled weakly as they made their way outside. They paused momentarily, looking up to the sky. The earlier drizzle had softened and now the sun almost threatened to breach the greyness above.

Sir Marmaduke Constable, a small, rotund and elderly Yorkshireman, was first to mount his horse and, accompanied by a ruddy-faced, taciturn Sir William Bulmer, set off with their guards down river where their division, made up of levies from Yorkshire's East Riding, and Durham, were camped furthest away, below Weetwood Moor. Meanwhile, following them, Lord Dacre, leader of the Borderers, and Lord Stanley, in charge of regiments from Lancashire and Cheshire, set off together, at first on foot, escorted and guarded by some of their knights, through the army's masses strewn across the flat ground covering the southern end of the widening valley floor.

Tired, damp and sullen-looking, the thousands that gathered in groups and huddles around smoky campfires or makeshift shelters appeared grey and disconsolate. Shortage of food and ale was beginning to undermine confidence and discipline. Mid-morning, four men from Durham, guilty of thieving rations the previous night, had been hanged from the branch of a large willow tree near the river and left dangling as a stark warning to others, tempted to rob from their fellow soldiers.

On their way to their respective contingents, both commanders were concerned by the mood of the troops, and they spoke words of encouragement as they passed. At a line of suffering men waiting to enter a physician's tent to have teeth pulled, Lord Dacre, by repute an austere and supercilious leader, ordered a swig of wine from his own provision to be given to each after his treatment. Likewise, the hard-faced Lord Stanley advised his aide to have a cask of honey delivered to the tent.

Unlike most camps where the men were kept busy to fill their time, chiefly training and practising skills of combat, there was little activity here as most of them had been on the march for many days and needed to rest and regain their strength. To occupy themselves, they simply sharpened, prepared and repaired weapons, armour and clothing; the only interruption a steady trail of sickly looking men across to long, shallow trenches that had been hurriedly dug for squatting over. The continual wet and cold weather had already caused widespread sickness and diarrhoea. If it were not for layers of wood smoke drifting through the camp, the stench would certainly have been fouler, adding to the general discomfort of all.

Conscious of the demands that would soon be upon them all in battle, a lulled state of gloom and foreboding had settled over the scene, like an executioner's hood.

8

Seth Milburn and his three brothers, 'Black' Bob, Dick and Samuel of Hepple Linn, in company with other men from the Elsdon area, were hunched in a circle, their fleece cloaks covering their frames. Rough and hardy men from the English Border country, they were used to survival as a way of life, and all had fought in skirmishes that resulted in wounding and death. It was a thrilling but fierce game in which feuding and revenge were commonplace. Despite the attempts of appointed Wardens and troops from both countries to control the extremes, it remained, to a large degree, lawless territory, dominated by the ties and mischief of family brotherhoods.

As well as Seth's brothers, there were other Milburns present – cousins and nephews, all hardy men, with two of their womenfolk and older men cooking and caring for them. Hundreds of camp followers like these were vital for the tasks and skills necessary in supporting such huge gatherings, and mostly they served their own communities. Although these Elsdon men were not trained, professional soldiers as a good number were in the English army, nevertheless they were tough fighters, born and bred to it by blood and nature, eager under Lord Dacre's command for vengeance and the spoils of victory.

Seth Milburn, the eldest of the four brothers, was broad-shouldered and powerful. He wielded a sword with such ferocity that no one cared to oppose him, even in sport. Like many men of prowess he assumed a quiet, assured manner that was admirable. His thick, curly brown hair framed a square-boned face with a dimpled chin. His nose, broken in wrestling and bare-knuckle fights when younger, added to the sternness of his expression. Yet, whenever amused and he smiled, his look at once radiated a happiness few others could muster. However, it seemed that no other emotion showed in between these two faces, which caused strangers to be a little wary of him.

"Man, if they think w' can fight on empty bellies then A'm off before any battle," 'Little' Lance Milburn moaned. Lance, an uncle to Seth and his brothers, came from Rothbury where he was famed as the best poacher on the River Coquet.

"We'll cut your legs off if y'u try," replied Davie Charlton, sitting beside him.

"He's short enough already, Davie," quipped 'Mossy' Charlton, his brother, who earlier in the year had married Seth's youngest sister, Jenny, who was also present cooking for them in camp.

"Well, maybe w' should cut off something else he hasn't put to good use yet, or likely will," joked Davie. This raised a laugh, for Lance, nearing fifty, had never married.

Lance elbowed Davie in the side. "Being married doesn't make a man a man. I've had more company of women than you've ever had, Davie lad, so hold your tongue."

Harry Milburn, a half-cousin from Otterburn, raised his gruff, bewhiskered face. "What kind o' man but a bald-headed coward would run from here leaving his kinsfolk," he cursed.

Devoid of any humour, the insult was intended. Lance gaped at grumpy Harry and for devilment scooped up a handful of mud and threw it carelessly at him. It hit his shoulder. The others laughed but quick tempered, Harry got to his feet, stepping forward in a rage. Seeing danger, Lance stood up ready to defend himself, but Seth moved swiftly, striding between them. "That's enough," he ordered. "Save your strength for the enemy and hold on t' your tempers. We're all sick of the rain and cold, and feeling edgy about what's comin'. But that's no reason to fall out. Now both of y'u shake hands an' forget it."

Lance showed he was willing, putting out his hand, but Harry spat on the ground in refusal of it. Seth grabbed him by the collar and drew him closer, glowering. "Do it, Harry," he said forcefully, then added the word 'please' to placate him. Harry's expression softened, but before he was able to comply, there was a stirring in the crowd, and men all around were rising to their feet and gathering to the blabber of news spreading through the ranks. The incident between the two Milburns dissolved at once as everyone around them joined an orderly drift of movement towards the avenue through the camp, leading to Surrey's headquarters.

Trailing through the masses, there appeared a column of some two hundred horsemen, at the head of which rode the outlaw Bastard Heron, conspicuously clad in black, and wearing his red cape. Behind him, on a silver horse, rode his 'second man', Hinson. Displaying their allegiance to Heron, each one of his riders wore a red kerchief tied round his neck.

As they drew nearer, a group of Border men began to cheer, and it expanded, growing louder and louder, like an incoming wave. Many of the riders were recognised, local heroes and villains alike; some related, some friends, some enemies. But the sight of them now, giving themselves up to join the force, appeared to relieve the despondency festering across the campsite, like welcome sunshine emerging between clouds to warm their backs.

Surprised by the commotion of support, John Heron reined-in his horse and peered round, still unsure. His eyes fell on Dacre's banners where a large tent was pitched, and he saw the commander with his knights striding sprightly towards him. Signalling for his followers to remain in the saddle, only he, Bastard Heron, dismounted.

Shortly, Lord Dacre confronted him with a steely regard. "So, John

Heron, we meet once more. Your surrender is brash to say the least, but timely to be sure."

"I do not surrender, my lord. I offer my help. And God knows it's needed," Heron stated bluntly.

Lord Dacre, Warden-General of the Marches, was not amused by the impertinence of the outlaw's reply. He was a friend to Sir William Heron, imprisoned for John Heron's crime, and cared little for the scoundrel and his troublesome past – his malice, treachery and disrespect of authority, flouting laws with reckless ease.

"In any other circumstance I would arrest you and see you hanged. However, our situation is perilous and your aid may prove gainful. Doubtless the Earl of Surrey has been alerted and is prepared for you. He will deal with you as he considers fit. My captains will see to your men. You, alone, will follow me on foot," he concluded haughtily, and walked on ahead towards the dwelling wherein the English commander-in-chief had, indeed, been awakened and informed of the outlaw Heron's arrival, accompanied by his cavalry of cutthroats and scoundrels.

Heron handed Hinson the reins of his horse and secretly cast him a look, communicating that Hinson be ready to act if help were needed. To acknowledge his leader's wish, Hinson made the customary sign, wiping the tip of his nose with his thumb. Satisfied, Heron turned and strode away, surrounded by soldiers, following Dacre's entourage.

9

When Heron entered the building his sword was taken from him, and he stood before Surrey who was already seated in an armchair, like some biblical judge. In silence each man appraised the other, sizing up one another's character, bearing, and attitude. Surrey perceived an agile, brooding figure, handsome yet menacing and with piercing, suspicious eyes. A man, Surrey surmised, of grim determination and obsessions. What Heron saw was a stout, elderly soldier who was naturally bold, confident and deeply mindful, his eyes alive and sharp.

"Can we trust you?" Surrey began, his voice calm.

Heron shifted his weight from one foot to the other, slightly bemused by this opening. "I shall fight for England with you against the invaders. You can trust me to do that."

Surrey smiled. "Can you trust yourself to do it?"

Again, John Heron found himself hesitating. "Of course," he answered, his voice aimed low, maintaining its balance.

Surrey pondered, his flint-sharp look trained on him. "How can you be faithful to England and its king when you break its law then run from it?"

Heron's reply was instant, without remorse. "I killed the Scottish Warden, Ker, in fairness for his crimes." His words were adamant. "My lord, I run from the law of Scotland, imposed upon England."

Surrey paused, his face hardening, and then he gave Heron a broad stare. "Many might argue with that, but well said. Any such agreement we once had with Scotland has now ceased." Surrey's tone sharpened. "But your Pardon is another matter, John Heron, remember that," he cautioned, his eyebrows raised. Shifting in his chair and turning to the room, Surrey announced an urgent meeting of his war council. Addressing Heron again, the old earl said, "I request that you remain here in attendance." And in a further gesture of faith and solidarity, Surrey instructed that the outlaw's sword be returned to him.

While the room was arranged and lesser figures departed, Heron stood for a moment, reflecting on Surrey's words and show of trust. He had heard about the man, his influence, his bravery, and his astuteness. But he hadn't been prepared to like him.

Soon, a large map of the area was rolled out across the table, showing this corner of northernmost England: Berwick down to Alnwick, across to Wooler and the Cheviot hills. Flodden Hill was marked with a circle and the roadways lined between the main villages. The River Till was also inked, snaking its way northwards to the larger River Tweed that separated the two countries.

It was obvious to John Heron why he was included in the meeting. A map could only tell so much. A map could not indicate where the ground tended to be wet or dry, or smooth or stony. It couldn't say where the short cuts ran across moors or through woods; where there was good spring water or an abundance of fruit or berries or birds' eggs. A map didn't show where deer liked to graze, or the pools and banks of rivers where fish were easily caught, and the places where it was dangerous or safe to cross. For strangers to the area, the map was limited. Surrey needed local knowledge, and knew there was no one better than a fugitive, born and raised here, who'd hunted, ventured, and ridden on horseback over every patch of ground.

With the old earl remaining seated, his elder son, Thomas, the admiral, stood to recount the possible course of action that they had proposed earlier. This entailed the ascent of Branxton Hill, north of Flodden – a choice forced upon them by the Scots' refusal to come down off the hill. From this height the dipped ground between the two armies was equal to both sides. Here, it seemed, a fair battle could be fought. However, to get there in time, beyond range of Scottish siege guns, would require a longer, arduous journey for an army already showing signs of fatigue and apathy. The broad-chested admiral, a younger version of his father in looks and manner, turned and fixed his eyes upon Heron.

"We need your knowledge and advice, John Heron. What be your thoughts on this strategy? What of the journey? How might we manage with artillery, horses, and men fully armed? Give us your opinion. Be candid." He paused to take a deep breath. "First, is it possible, and next, what is the most practical, suitable way for us to go, delaying the Scots?" he demanded.

Bastard Heron agreed that it was achievable but that it was not possible to march round in a single day before fighting a battle. Therefore, they would need to leave tomorrow, Wednesday, or possibly Thursday. Leaning over the map, he studied it closely. He placed the tip of his forefinger beside Wooler. "We are here. To head north we must cross the Till *there*, at the ford to Doddington, and *here*, at Weetwood Bridge. Clearly, with the water higher than usual from all the rain, the artillery shall use the narrow bridge. At the ford, troops will need to link arms so as not to lose their footing. The current is much stronger than is usual at this time of year."

He paused and looked hesitantly at the admiral, who nodded his approval. Heron continued. "Over the river there is a rough, solid road through the hamlet, climbing uphill over Doddington Moor to reach Barmoor, eight miles from Wooler. On the way we shall be out of range of their large guns and be out of sight from Flodden, with the ridge, here, above Fenton providing cover."

Admiral Howard angled himself over the map. "Perhaps we might camp overnight somewhere along the Berwick road so that Scottish spies may judge it to be our destination, thus concealing our intention to circle round, behind Flodden." He glanced up at Heron. "Where would you recommend that we pass the night?" he asked.

Heron pointed to an area just north of Barmoor Tower. There, he told them, lay firm ground, slightly raised and sheltered by a scattering of trees and bushes, and with pure-water springs nearby. A supply of drinkable water was essential since he had heard that beer rations were low. "Thirst can defeat a man long before hunger," he emphasised with calm authority.

The commanders glanced at one another. Only Dacre and Bulmer knew something of Heron's background and of his wild, violent, wolfish ways. They'd anticipated that he'd be cunning and wary, but in their presence his quiet assurance and intelligence impressed them. Perhaps the reaction of the mob that greeted his arrival was more meaningful than they had comprehended at the time?

The Lord Admiral seated himself and now his father, the Earl of Surrey, leaned forward to speak, his thick-veined hands grasping the table's edge. "After spending the night at Barmoor," he explained, "we shall need to rise early on the day of battle. Our army shall march westward from Bowsden, and onward past Duddo to reach the river. To cross the Till again, the artillery will require the bridge at Twizel." He stared confidently at Heron. "Since we shall be pressed for time, we request that you indicate those fords upstream that other regiments might wade."

Heron placed his forefinger on the map at the location of the Millford at Heaton, then traced upstream to Etal, and finally to Willowford and Sandyford on the river's bend, near the village of Crookham. "These are the common crossing places and, considering the level of high water, the safest."

Once more, he urged that caution be heeded in the strong current. "The River Till," he stressed, "has a reputation for drowning and is nicknamed 'the Kill River' by local folk."

Dacre interrupted, asking Heron if he knew the local rhyme that he himself had recently heard regarding its danger. Heron confirmed that he did. "Then I ask that you recite the saying for us," Dacre said, folding his arms in smug expectation.

Heron stared, realising that Dacre's request was simply a ruse to test his local knowledge. Should he be unable to remember the words, no doubt Dacre would enjoy the moment. Not to be undermined, Heron rolled out the verse without hesitation: "Tweed says to Till, why does your water flow so still? Till says to Tweed, though you have speed, far quicker than me, for every one you drown, I'll kill three." Somewhat self-conscious of his effort, Heron shrugged, to the mild amusement of his audience.

Surrey sat back, grinning. "Well said. And then after we cross the river, what of our way to Branxton?"

Heron replied explaining that once they reached higher ground they would turn left and then head southwards to Pallinsburn. "At Pallinsburn, a long stretch of marshland lies in our way," he cautioned. "The bulk of the army will have to skirt around it, but, to save time, a narrow causeway known hereabouts as the Branx Brig could take the artillery across." To confirm their attention, Heron's eyes roamed from face to face. He continued briskly, "On the other side of the bog and bank of the dene, the ground rises towards the village, followed by a short ascent and then a down slope leading to a long, steep climb onto Branxton Hill. From the top," he emphasised, "Flodden sits a mile away, across a shallow moor."

Surrey cleared his throat to speak. "And tell me, John Heron, how far is the journey from Barmoor to Branxton Hill by way of Twizel?" he prompted.

Heron squinted towards the ceiling and faintly nodded as if counting. "A little over thirteen miles," he reckoned. "It is close enough, but on soggy ground it will be tougher for men to march and then have energy to fight." His eyes narrowed and a scowl of defiance knotted his face. "They shall have need of leaders that inspire them!" he added finally, charging the noblemen before him.

As a gesture of gratitude, the Earl of Surrey heaved himself up, and onto his feet. He addressed Heron formally and warmly. "I thank you for your information and advice. I wish now to speak with my commanders. Go to your men and see that they are settled. Remember, only we in this room know of this plan. It must not pass any of our lips. Tempted by reward, there are some in the camp who would gladly inform the Scots of it. That would prove disastrous," he concluded solemnly.

John Heron gave a slight bow, returning the grace afforded him, and then, unaccompanied, he departed the room. Eyes gleaming, the heartening words of the general glowed in the outlaw's thoughts as he stepped outside to be met by his four main men, 'Cuddy' Hinson, Joe Telfer, Straughen – 'the big one', and 'Badger' Weatherburn, all allied to Heron since boyhood.

10

At the age of twelve, already deemed an outcast and troublesome in his own circle, Heron had been out riding upriver from Ford, near Ewart, hunting with his falcon, when he came across a group of four rough-looking country boys about his own age. Sons of labourers, the noisy gang was at play, sword fencing with wooden sticks. They ignored him at first, sitting on his pony at the edge of the meadow, and continued their practice.

Young Heron remained watching from a distance. They did not recognise him but knew he was not their sort. One of them, the lad who could lithely handle the biggest boy's hefty strikes, walked towards him. His mouth was small and serious but his eyes were friendly. He stroked the nervous pony's nose to calm it. The boy said his name was Cuthbert Hinson, Cuddy for short, and invited the young rider to come closer and watch their game more easily. His openness was appealing.

Heron remained in the saddle and, without speaking, followed him towards the group. Quite happily, they introduced themselves to him. The small, stocky boy with a grin was called Joe Telfer, the tallest and strongest was Straughen, and the last to speak was Adam Weatherburn, who regarded the young horseman with a merry glint. Heron observed the unnatural grey streak in his mop of rust-brown hair.

"You have a real sword," pointed Hinson. "Have y'u been taught t' use it?"

John Heron told them he'd had lessons for a few years.

"Will you teach us? We'll give you things if y'u do," Hinson added eagerly.

Young Heron wanted to smile but didn't. "What are *things*?" he asked.

"We'll give y'u what you ask for," declared Weatherburn. "There's no need givin' y'u what y'u don't want!"

Heron revealed himself with a small chuckle, and they did, too. "I'll come here tomorrow at this time," he announced. "We'll use sticks until you're good enough. Agreed?"

"Aye!" they cried happily and waved him off as he turned and rode away at a gallop.

When he'd gone they looked gladly at each other. "We forgot to ask his name," said Joe Telfer suddenly, with a frown.

"He didn't tell us, either," remarked Hinson, eyes gleaming.

Stirred by their enthusiasm, young Heron kept his word, and asked for nothing. He proved to be a good teacher, showing them the basic moves in attack and defence using wrist and arm. He complained that they did not use their feet well enough for balance and drilled them accordingly. Although he was patient and convivial towards them, even now and again showing slight humour, there remained a division between himself and the common youths that was more than the mere status of his being a nobleman's son; a detachment that constrained him like an invisible chain.

They very soon learned that he was not one to upset and at times a streak of anger shaded his eyes, making them feel wary of his temper. Foolishly, Straughen once tripped him up when being shown a move and Heron sprang to his feet in fury, viciously whacking him on the shoulder before the big boy could block it. "It'll be your head next time," hissed Heron as Straughen, his face contorted, squirmed in pain.

Without acting superior, he assumed leadership and they learned to accept it. They soon found out who he was and of his mother's death, which led to him living with his father's family at Ford Castle. Joe Telfer's grandmother whispered that Heron was a strange kind of boy, with the Devil's blood in him. A vile youth, full of spite, another said, and one that they should stay away from. But for the lads from Ewart, these warnings only served to enrich their fascination and their willingness to be especially loyal to him.

When Heron was of an age, his father, Roger Heron, appointed his bastard son to take up residence at Crawley Tower near Powburn, a place eight miles south of Wooler. His allowance was meagre. To supplement his earnings, Heron began to venture, raiding into Scotland, gaining from what he stole. Raiding or 'reiving' as it was known, was a maligned but accepted practice throughout the Borderland. The boys he'd trained to swordfight, now young men like himself, became his close followers and they enjoyed the adventure and the rewards of their plundering.

To ensure their fitness to ride and fight, Heron demanded that they practise and exercise. He implemented a regime of military drills to develop skills and stamina so that they were athletic and tough enough for the rigours of their trade. Heron led by example, applying himself to the routines with demonic vigour, inspiring others to become, like him, trained combatants. Furthermore, their horses, the best of their kind, were ridden most days so that they remain in top condition, capable of covering long distances or achieving short bursts of speed over rough, hilly terrain.

Heron's infamy amongst Scottish folk was quickly conjured by his daring, ruthless exploits and, before long, he and his growing band of marauders, identified by the red neckerchiefs they wore, were feared and hated for their barbarism. After his part in the treacherous murder of the Scottish Warden, Robert Ker, his enemies swore revenge and hired killers sought in vain to reach the elusive Heron. Guarded by his henchmen, local thieves, and families who occasionally sheltered him, Heron's notoriety spread throughout the region. He seemed untouchable, like a phantom in the moon's eerie light.

11

After the Scottish herald, Islay, had ridden down from Flodden Hill to deliver his king's message to the English camp at Wooler, King James returned pensively to his table to write another letter. Two guards stood inside the doorway. He strained to find meaningful words to express himself and, thinking the two soldiers were a distraction, he ordered them outside. Alone, he felt it easier to speak freely onto the page. Controlling the cries leaping from his heart, his face maintained a mask of calm concentration as his words scratched onto the page.

'Dearest Lady Elizabeth, I am haunted by the rudeness of my conduct when leaving you at Ford Castle. Despite the heavy responsibility that burdens me, as we prepare for battle with the English, I allowed myself the meanest urge to torment and belittle you as though you were but a common servant. I meekly admit that it was uncivil and offensive. Even as I write to you now, the shame of it sears my heart. How insensitive and disgraceful I revealed myself before your person, and I pray that you deign to accept my deepest, humblest apology.

On Friday, three days from now, we are due to confront the English. I am fully ready to front my army into battle. We have prepared thoroughly and are in good spirits. Our guns are set in place, our pike formations suitably trained by our French comrades, and, thanks to God, there is a belief building in us that the conflict will end quickly in our favour. We are excited by the prospect of a swift, convincing victory.

Our spies report that all is not well with the English. Unlike our forces, their soldiers are weary, disconsolate and hungry, and sickness rages through their camp. We have learned that dissent is spreading its wings among their regiments. There is also a rumour that they may not fight at all, fearful of our superiority. God willing that it would be so. Had King Henry acted reasonably and relented earlier upon his decision to invade France, I assure you none of this would be.

As agreed, orders have been delivered to Edinburgh regarding the imminent release of your husband, Sir William, from Fast Castle. Nevertheless, my dearest, you ought know that I crave your company as much as your pardon. In truth, my soul will not be satisfied until we hold hands again. In you, fair Elizabeth, I find a love unlike any other. I dream constantly of your beauty, your tenderness and affection. When this conflict is over I promise to make arrangements for you to join me where and whenever it is possible.

To prove that you receive this letter and accept my apology, I ask that you send in return, with a servant you trust, the small opal brooch that was fastened to your tunic jacket, and which, if you remember, I so admired.'

He raised the quill and read through his words again then signed it simply with a capital 'J', omitting any reference to his name and title. Having sealed it himself, he called an aide to have it delivered to three horsemen summoned to ride at once, and handed over a pouch of coins to pay them and whomever they hired from within the walls of Berwick.

12

On the eastern slope of Flodden Hill a group of Teviotdale men, mostly Taits and Burns, chewed lumps of mutton that they plucked from a large, steaming cauldron suspended over burning logs. There was a fine, misty drizzle, no wind, and a feeble orb of sun perched in a slate-coloured, late afternoon sky. The group, numbering some forty men, was on its feet, hovering around the fire like crows round a carcass, happily feeding. Their heavy woven clothes and leather jackets were shabby with damp and dirt, adding to their rough, wild, shadowy appearance.

Under Home, the Border lord, they were eager to fight the enemy. Their history of raiding, robbery and murder was as notorious as that of their English counterparts whom they loathed and sought with perpetual vengeance. Each one of them there carried a personal grudge of some sort and was outspoken about it.

"If A'm killed m'sel', taking three or more Ogles wi' me, I'll have no complaint," 'Tickler' Tait growled in his cousin Andrew's ear. He'd earned his nickname from his ability to catch fish by hand, stroking their bellies before grabbing them by the gills.

"Aim for thirty-three, man, an' songs will be sung about y'u for evermore," Andrew replied, jovially.

Tickler grinned at the mad possibility of it. "Now if Aa was in charge of one o' them muckle guns Aa maybe could." His weathered face cracked happily at the thought.

The power and size of the king's cannon, already demonstrated in battering Norham Castle into submission, had many a Scot believing the English army would never get within a mile of Flodden before turning tail, to run away in terror.

Andrew Tait, a big, heavy-set man with long, dark, straggled hair, turned to his friend on his other side, a tall, gangling, bony-faced individual called Jock Burn, a member of another large frontier family. Jock had with him four sons, the youngest only thirteen. One younger boy was still at home with their mother and two sisters, to take care of the cows, pigs and sheep. The thirteen-year-old, Ewan, had been left at home too, but was determined to fight alongside his father and three brothers and had sneaked into camp two days earlier. His courage was celebrated amongst the Border troops as a positive omen and his father, Jock, was a proud man because of it.

"Now, Jock," began Andrew, "Aa hear the French count isn't happy with the way we Border men scoff at his French soldiers trying t' train us with the long spears. He's said to have asked Bothwell to order us to obey their instruction or be flogged. What do y'u think of that?"

Jock wiped his mouth with the back of his hand and snorted. "Bothwell's no fool. When it comes t' fightin' he knows we're his best men. Nay family here will let one o' their own be beaten without a riot. Bothwell kens that much."

Andrew's younger brother, Archie, an acclaimed horse rider, swordsman and gambler, who had earlier in the year joined the Kers in an unsuccessful hunt for Bastard Heron, pushed forward to fork a chunk of meat from the pot. In his early twenties, he was good looking to a point of beauty and women swooned at the sight of him, whilst men admired his nerve and mischievous nature. He glanced at them with an eager smirk. Nearly all the Taits possessed blue-green eyes that sparkled when excited. Even when older, like Tickler who was in his late forties, the cast of their eyes remained youthful. Archie, a daredevil joker, clearly had something to tell them.

"What d' you reckon t' this bet, men," he began loudly, wanting others nearby to hear as well, "that Aa canna go t' the Rutherfords and beg some wine from them?"

Andrew's stare was sharp enough to look through him. "They'll yank your guts out before y'u know it. They loathe us Taits as much as the' hate the Kers."

Archie laughed. "The group over there, mostly Youngs from Hawick, have a five-shilling bet together that Aa'd be too feared t' do it."

Andrew and Tickler looked at each other. Archie was as crafty as a cuckoo. They suspected there was more to it and asked him to continue. Squinting at them, he said he needed someone on a pony ready to ride in and pick him up if things went wrong. They shook their heads at once, dismissing the idea as madness.

"Two shillings if you have t' come to ma aid," he tempted them. Without hesitation Tickler's brother, George 'Wouldhave' Tait, butted in, saying he would happily do it for that amount. "But how will Aa ken if y'u want me t' come to your rescue?" he demanded with a frown.

His cousin Archie chuckled. "When the spears go in one side and come oot the other," he joked, then clapped Wouldhave on the shoulder and beckoned him away from the crowd to talk it over, disappearing into the throng uphill and away from their companions, who continued munching meat round the smoky fire.

To ensure there was no deception, one of the Youngs who'd bet the money was nominated to witness Archie entering the Rutherford camp and see him come out, with or without the wine. As this fellow, a round, jolly, baggy-eyed character called Robbie Young, stood with the rest of the Taits and Burns lingering in expectation, waiting for Archie and Wouldhave to return, a sense of excitement trickled over into neighbouring sections of the camp. Of course, it didn't take long before that part of the slope was simmering with amused interest, creating a welcome diversion from the boredom and dreariness of camp life.

Eventually, when Wouldhave returned, he was alone. Hurriedly collecting Robbie Young, the two of them trailed away together, presumably to meet up with Archie whose absence had already raised suspicion in a few family members.

"He better no' be cheatin' the Youngs," muttered Andrew.

Tickler snorted. "He'll not cheat them, but he's no' daft enough t' think he can walk past the Rutherfords without them blockin' 'is way."

Pausing beside a makeshift shelter of skins draped over wooden poles, a young woman approached, leading a tan-coloured pony, which she handed over to Wouldhave, who said nothing. Wearing a long woollen skirt that trailed the ground, and a dark cloak hanging from her shoulders to her knees, she turned to Robbie. A shawl covered her head and was strung round her neck framing her face, with a sleek curve of black hair falling over one cheek. Her gleaming blue-green eyes and proud, distant look made her attractive in an uncommon way.

"Let's go, then" she said, and Robbie Young's baggy eyes widened. It was Archie's voice.

"Aye, it's me. I said Aa'd do it and do it Aa will."

Robbie emitted a mighty laugh, shaking his head in amused wonder. "Y'u make a bonny lassie, Archie Tait, I'll give you that. But it's cheating, is it no'?"

"I said Aa'd do it. Aa didn't say how," Archie answered, remonstrating the fact and went on to explain how his sister, here in the camp working as a cook, had helped him to get ready, scraping off his few whiskers and lending him clothes.

Robbie chuckled. "Well, I'm not going t' argue with y'u, though the others might. But A'm happy to see if y'u get away with it."

Together, side-by-side, they followed the path around the slope, teeming with soldiers, until they arrived at the site occupied by the Rutherford family, a brazen, aggressive clan, infamously bent on dispute and reprisal. Leaving Robbie and Wouldhave to watch him from a safe distance, Archie, in disguise, circled round the huddles of men and their fires, towards a canopied wagon where one man stood in charge, clearly guarding their provisions.

Archie spoke to the guard, telling him, in his most beguiling feminine voice, how his father was sick and unable to drink any beer without vomiting, and how desperate his thirst was becoming; that they had no wine, and maybe he could stomach it better than beer and it would surely save him from certain death. But the guard shook his head. Archie appeared to cover his face, pretending to sob, and then leaned closer to the guard and whispered in his ear. The man hesitated and then pawed his way into the wagon, and came out handing over a small bag, which Archie promptly concealed beneath his cloak. Slowly turning, he made his way back to where Robbie and Wouldhave were anxiously waiting, and walked past them as if they weren't there, in case anyone watching suspected some sort of trickery. Out of sight of the Rutherfords, Archie stopped and turned round, his face beaming. "It was easier than Aa thought."

"What did you say to change the man's mind, Archie?" demanded Wouldhave.

"I nibbled his ear and said Aa'd come back later t' find him and show how thankful Aa was," he said, in his woman's voice.

They guffawed in fits all the way back to their own camp where Archie, surrounded by a large crowd, revealed himself and the small bag of wine he'd been given. To a man, at Robbie Young's insistence, the joke was well received by the losers and they paid up. Consequently, on that section of the hillside, the madcap Archie and his outrageous prank mooned over everyone's mind as they settled down for the night, clutching their rations of beer and coverings against the coming of another watery, chilly night.

13

On the western side of Flodden Hill, in King James's grand pavilion circled by banners and his household guards, an early evening meeting with his war council had been called to report on the army's training and the day's affairs. Four spluttering torches threw flickering light across the arc of earnest looking individuals seated on padded benches. Present were James's natural son – Alexander Stewart, the Archbishop of Saint Andrews; George Hepburn, Bishop of the Isles; the earls of Huntly, Lennox, Argyll, Angus, Bothwell, Errol, Crawford, Montrose, Casillis, Morton, and Rothes; the lords – Home, Herries, Borthwick, Maxwell, Innermeath and Sempill, plus the French Count d'Aussi, a slim, neatly dressed man with dark ringlets of hair hanging over his shoulders.

Soldiers brought in the English herald, Thomas Hawley. In response to his being held as a hostage at Flodden, the Scottish herald, Islay, had not returned from Wooler. King James felt it was no longer necessary to extend the measure. He instructed the English messenger to return to his master and to advise him, informally, that the Scottish army was determined to remain on Flodden Hill and would fight the English on Friday, as agreed.

"As you can observe," James addressed the round-faced English herald, "we are steadfast in heart and mind and our confidence grows by the hour. Be sure to inform him of this," King James declared with ceremonial air to amuse his nobles. With a summary flick of his hand he dismissed the portly emissary, who acted his part, bowing graciously before he went.

Following Rouge Croix's departure, the king invited the French count to explain why it was that the pike columns must advance in silence, for it was unnatural to the Scots. In a vain, exaggerated English accent, irksome to some in the company, the count justified the tactic as essential to the concentration required for keeping tight formation. Citing the names of continental battles no one else present had heard of, he assured his audience that compact, disciplined pike divisions had already proven invincible.

"Silence itself is a weapon also," Count d'Aussi asserted, "like a ship slowly turning sideways before firing its guns, planting fear into its enemy." He paused looking for satisfaction in the eyes of his audience and, seeing none, went on to say that his captains were full of praise for the Scottish soldiers in their training and that they were ready to overpower the English ranks.

Reassured, King James thanked the count, speaking in fluent French, and then continued with the meeting, asking that individual reports of his troops' preparations be recounted. Lord Maxwell, known for his languid and overblown way of speaking, began. "It is my pleasure to inform you that the ailment of coughing and sickness that has been detrimental to many of our soldiers, as it grew and spread through the camp, seems to have abated and is no longer a concern. I believe we..." King James cut in to thank him, and then indicated for the next to speak. Aware of their king's impatience, one after the other of his senior commanders delivered brief, positive comments, describing confidence in their soldiers' readiness and their rigorous self-belief in defeating the enemy. "There is, Your Majesty," Montrose admitted cheerily at the close of his summation, "a pride in what we represent that emanates throughout the ranks."

Concluding the business, King James expressed his delight at his army's commitment and lauded their endeavours. "It is an honour for us, my trusty nobles, to lead an army of such magnitude and potential. We have the resources and resolve to be triumphant. Our country shall not be subdued by English persuasion. We shall not step aside for its young, bullish king. Let each one of us hereby vow that King Henry shall learn to respect and revere our nation." James's tone and manner revealed how his appetite for combat was stronger than ever. Reaching a high note of passion, he venerated his commanders again for their service and loyalty to the cause.

Suddenly his expression hardened. "I have, however, something to say now that disturbs me greatly." The room stilled.

He straightened in his seat, raising his chin, his hands clasped in his lap. Loosening his grip, he gently tugged at the turquoise ring on his finger. Earlier, in a private meeting, he had been disappointed with the Earl of Angus and his continuing scepticism. Now seemed the right moment to exercise his authority and consolidate his power of leadership. He summoned the elderly Angus forward, to stand before his king, and stated firmly how vexed he was with the old man's opposing view of the conflict; one that he stubbornly and foolishly maintained. King James announced, with a look of contempt, that he would not tolerate it any longer since it undermined the resolution of his army's intent.

"There is no place here for a heart that flutters," he rebuked Angus, scornfully.

The old earl swallowed, taken aback by the sudden vindictiveness of his king. Hurt blanked his face. "May I speak, Sire?" he asked. The king gave the slightest of nods. "As I earlier expressed to Your Majesty, I do not fear the fight; I fear the consequences of it." Though his voice sounded brittle, his words were precise. "With victory we may rescue France for a short while, but Scotland will soon suffer the wrath of young King Henry, and of all England. It is certain. I honestly believe we have nothing to gain by this conflict; a conflict, some believe, inspired chiefly by foreign bidding."

King James cut him down savagely. "I have heard these excuses before and I have had enough of your complaint. Since you clearly distrust my judgement and fail to understand the purpose and importance of our alliance with France, I therefore command that you to leave this camp by morning and return to your home. This is no place and time for you, or any other," he paused, looking around, "whose hand I cannot grip!" He stared into Angus's eyes, moistening with tears at the tone of his king's scolding. "My decision is final. I order you to go from us now," James stated, vehemently. "At once!" he shouted.

Dejected, the old earl bowed his head. "Both my sons shall remain to fight in the field along with others in my service," he dared to add, his voice creaking with emotion. "I pray that God will prove my fears unfounded and the battle bears us no ill."

Slowly, achingly, Archibald Douglas, Earl of Angus, turned and with shoulders slumped, he retreated from the king's room with his head lowered. For a few, almost deafening moments, a baleful silence quivered in the flames' glare before King James addressed them again, with renewed vigour. Members of the council were, by now, used to his swings of mood, a feature of his current disposition.

"Lord Home," he exhorted loudly, "tell us again of those Englishmen who have joined us this day from Surrey's camp, and how we hear that his army's resolve dwindles each day with hunger, thirst and discontent."

With an assured swagger, Lord Home paraded the floor while King James, eyes dazzling, gloated once more over the news of some thirty English Borderers, men related to the Scottish Halls of Heavyside, who had given themselves up at dawn that morning. They had spoken, also, of the great disquiet among the English soldiers and how many more like them were ready to cross sides if they could. Furthermore, they had reported a whispering throughout the English ranks of the suspicion that the Earl of Surrey, at seventy, appeared too old and infirm to successfully lead an army.

Holding a goblet of fine French wine, a gift from the Count d'Aussi, James relaxed back in his chair as Home's words soothed the strain of his confrontation with the Earl of Angus. Angus, the man who had cared for him from boyhood, who'd stood by him through the years, supporting, aiding and guiding him to be the king he now was. Angus, a lifelong ally, praising and encouraging him almost like a father, until of late.

****

Patrick Lindsay, Lord of the Byres, waited until darkness smothered the hill before he made his way unseen to the old earl's tent, guarded by household soldiers from his home in Fife. Seated listlessly in his chair, Archibald Douglas permitted him to enter and wearily stood to meet his friend.

Lindsay, a tiny figure with thin red hair and a prominent, tapered jaw that made his head seem oversized, stared in pity at the broken look that warped the earl's face. Lindsay and others were fearful, too, of the consequence of the king's decision to invade, but had yet to declare it openly as the Earl of Angus had done.

"I've come to offer my sympathy and my regret for the shame and humiliation cast upon you. I can see the pain it causes you. Be assured that I and others will, beyond Flodden and the battle, do all in our power to reinstate your good self with our king and his favour."

Archibald Douglas, tears visible, thanked him earnestly. "I am indebted to you for your consideration and the hope it offers. Although I spoke that which I believe to be true, it is only at the king's understanding and forgiveness that I shall feel again true to Scotland."

Lindsay glanced sideways, left and right, then leaned closer to secretly confide his thoughts. "No one doubts your loyalty to our own country," he argued. "King James persists in wearing the French queen's ring on his little finger – where it fits. He displays and fondles it as an emblem of reliance and principle. But it does not signify or represent the land of our birth for which we have gathered. It speaks not for Scotland as you have done."

Angus paused, reflecting on Lindsay's courage to express words that were, beyond this shelter, treasonable. He drew breath. "I cannot say more, other than I shall pray hourly that it does not become a ring of regret... a ring of sorrow."

The two men stared at each other. Angus sighed, as though a dying man. Formally, they embraced. Then Patrick Lindsay turned and, with furtive steps, made his exit, leaving the banished earl alone to bear his misery like a spike in his chest.

14

On the Wednesday, late morning, John Heron was summoned to meet Lord Dacre at Surrey's headquarters.

The earl was himself absent, touring in his open carriage through his troops, meeting officers responsible for the organisation and welfare of the common soldiers. Despite his age and condition, and climbing down from his transport with difficulty, Surrey was an inspiration to all those around him. In his company, doubters were quickly converted by his doughtiness and humour. He also had a special knack of remembering faces and names that endeared him to the lower ranks, which he never by-passed without words of encouragement, while his self-belief and calm objectivity instilled confidence among his chiefs, his captains and sergeants.

At the meeting, Heron found himself faced by Lord Dacre, a glowering Sir William Bulmer, and William Percy. Percy, a tall, distinguished looking, fair-haired knight, had hunted several times in the Cheviot Hills and was acquainted with Sir William Heron, though not with his infamous half-brother. William Percy began by informing Bastard Heron of news he'd received in haste from Alnwick – that a family of felons, Forsters from south Northumberland, had arrived with three wagons of food supplies, intent on profiting from the fleeing populace that had descended upon the town. These carriages had been identified as part of the wagon train intended for the English army and which thieves had ambushed.

Following this information, Dacre instructed Heron, with a dozen or so of his toughest men, to ride at once for Alnwick, to rescue the wagons and deal with the robbers. His face narrowed. "Perhaps," he added sardonically, "this be an opportunity for you, Heron, to prove yourself worthy of your allegiance to the Earl of Surrey, and of the faith shown by the general towards you."

Lord Thomas Dacre of Gilsland, Warden of the West Marches, at forty-six years old was an aristocratic, abrasive leader. Head of a powerful, wealthy Border family with a fiercely uncompromising reputation, he felt uneasy about the homage Heron received from the Howards, in view of his past crimes, his contempt for the law and of those in authority who administered it. Furthermore, like the dour-faced Bulmer, he disdained the hero status that accompanied the Bastard's name along the English Border – an image Dacre thought wholly undeserved.

John Heron ignored the sarcasm and responded to the challenge with a faint, wry smile followed by an affirmative nod of his head. However much Dacre tried to antagonise him, he refused to succumb. Before departing he glanced at the slanted eyes of Bulmer, Deputy Warden of the English East March, whose attempts to capture Heron had been continually thwarted. A morose Bulmer had remained silent throughout the meeting, extending his enmity and suspicion of the outlaw who'd outrun him these past years.

****

Within the next hour, accompanied by eleven of his most reliable and fiercest of men – Hinson, Straughen, Weatherburn, both Telfers, Hedley,

Thompson and the four Dunne brothers from Kyloe, John Heron, red cape flapping, led the way, riding at a canter along the puddled dirt road south of Wooler. Five miles on, having forded the River Till at Bewick Mill, they continued through Eglingham where the few nervous villagers that remained ran to hide. Crossing a drenched, windswept Shipley Moor, they eventually reached the boundary of Alnwick by mid-afternoon.

Outside the town's walls, in the pastures below the Percy stronghold of Alnwick Castle, hundreds of families had taken refuge in a temporary campsite. Earlier, in August, when the Scottish army had advanced towards the Border into north Northumberland, the fearful, outlying population had hurriedly gathered up the belongings, provisions and livestock they were able to take with them and, in droves, left their hamlets and villages to trek to the garrisoned safety of Berwick, Bamburgh, or Alnwick. Those who had relatives within the towns sought accommodation with them, while the majority made shelters outside the walls, knowing that at the threat of danger the gates would be open to them.

Reaching the River Aln, Heron and his dauntless band of men skirted round the town of Alnwick, following the left bank of the river, to arrive at the wooden bridge below the hill on which stood the great castle. In the huge field next to the river, row upon row of rough shelters and tents housed the hundreds of displaced families. Dismounting, Heron was seen to exchange his riding gloves for sword gauntlets, specially designed with metal strips to protect his hands. Leaving their mounts tethered to trees near the bridge, he quickly divided his party into four groups of three and, to avoid attention, each moved off separately along churned, muddy pathways through the squalid, battered existence of disrupted lives.

They'd travelled only a short distance when it became evident, from a sullen gathering of people, where the supply wagons were stationed. Heron signalled for the others to hold back while he and his two main bodyguards, Cuddy Hinson and the big man, Straughen, forced their way forward to the front of the queue. The gang of men in charge of the business of dishing out rations and receiving payment, stopped to stare at the three troopers standing brazenly before them. Behind them, the crowd was agitated, muttering unhappily at the strangers' intervention. An older fellow, from his appearance clearly the father of the ruffians, scowled at them. He had a greying, bushy beard and a wide-nosed, hostile face. Deliberately, his six mean-looking sons gripped the handles of their short swords and knives.

"What d' y'u want?" the man growled at the sword-carrying figure that stepped to the fore. Dressed in black and with a red cape across his shoulders, Heron's aspect was commanding.

Bastard Heron confronted him with a cold stare as he replied, "We want everything," he demanded. "How much do you want for the lot, including the wagons?"

The bearded man smirked. He thought there were only three of them. "Two hundred shillings," he replied, ridiculously. He pulled a face as a show of reason. "But then, what'll these poor folks have t' say, if y'u buy everythin' an' leave 'em hungry, eh?"

"The English army at Wooler is short of food and drink. Their need comes first," declared Heron, loud enough for the crowd to hear him. The man hesitated. The tip of his tongue circled his mouth, as if clearing the way for him to speak and his voice coarsened. "W' know nothin' of that, if it's right. But Aa cannot see the three of y'u getting back t' the road past everyone." He leaned forward. "Aa would leave if Aa was you, before the's any trouble," he warned, his face close enough for Heron to smell his stale breath and study the evil in his eyes.

Heron seemed unperturbed by the threat. He used his thumb to stroke the end of his nose and deliberately gazed past the man, as if considering the warning. Hinson and Straughen knew what was coming.

Suddenly, as fast as a striking snake, Heron snatched the villain by the beard and yanked him violently about, into a hold. Before the sons could react, he'd whipped out the man's knife and held the point to his exposed throat.

"Don't move closer or I'll slice his gizzard open!" snapped Heron as the rest of his own men swooped onto the scene, arrows ready in their crossbows. The gaping crowd drew back in alarm and the Bastard's name was heard aloud. "Tell your boys to drop their weapons and I promise, no blood will be shed," Heron commanded. "All we want is the wagons and their loads. I'll say it again, obey and no blood will be spilt. You have my word."

Wickedly twisting the man's beard, he forced a reply. "Do what he says," the man rasped, grimacing in agony.

Dropping their knives and short swords onto the ground, the man's sons were ordered to kneel as Hinson, Weatherburn and Joe Telfer tied their arms behind their backs. "W' don't want y'u comin' straight after us, do we?" explained Cuddy Hinson, securing the knots and helping each one in turn back onto his feet.

While the four Dunne brothers, Hedley and Thompson were left to hitch the wagons, preparing them for the journey back to Wooler, the prisoners were escorted in single file along the path nearest the river's bank. Halfway back towards the bridge they halted, and Heron instructed that all seven of the family be tied together into a cluster so that it would be harder for them to break loose.

"We'll get y'u for this," one of the sons snarled from the pack, his scowl vile and spiteful. Then he spat. Heron just managed to avoid it, shielding his face with a gloved hand.

John Heron stared. "Now why would you want to do that?" he asked calmly, stepping closer into the man's evil glare. "I promised no blood would be shed and I've kept my word, haven't I?"

He paused, his dark eyes narrowing before he added the fatal words. "That is, until now!" And immediately, he launched a vicious punch into the other's face, his metal-lined gauntlet smashing the man's head backwards. Trussed to the rest of the group, he could not fall and remained on his feet. He gawped dizzily, semi-conscious, his upper lip gashed with two brown teeth dangling in a bubble of oozing blood. Turning away from the individual, Heron carelessly walked away with Hinson, Weatherburn, Telfer and his younger brother, known as 'Skinner', leaving only Straughen behind with the prisoners.

Straughen grinned at the robbers, who glanced uncertainly about, silently confused by only his remaining behind with them. Still facing them, Straughen backed away several steps, paused, and then with a mighty roar, he charged into them like a bullock, bowling them over the bank into the swollen, murky current. And like a big, rolling log, the bundle of shrieking, drowning men was swept away downstream. From the bank side, Straughen watched them go and chuckled.

A group of children from the camp who had been watching proceedings from a short distance, set off running along the bank, yelping excitedly, as if seeing some bizarre form of entertainment. The knot of prisoners disappeared and then rose to the surface, feet kicking, thrashing, carried along by the flood into a deep, swirling pool where they vanished again – the gurgle and splash of water quickly terminating their cries.

Minutes later, the twelve troopers reassembled where they'd left the horses and prepared to leave with the cattle-drawn wagons. Before he mounted his horse, Heron gathered his men round to share out the coins that he had confiscated from the robber's purse. Finally, he addressed them all. "I have a letter to deliver to the castle from William Percy to his sister. Hinson will take charge of you on the journey back to camp. Make haste, men, there's little more than two hours' daylight left. A good many more English soldiers will eat better tonight because of you." Then, climbing up onto his speckled roan horse he left them, crossing over the wooden bridge that led uphill to the town.

Watching him depart, his men grinned knowingly amongst themselves, though aware that it was tactful to say nothing. In charge, Hinson ordered the twin brothers, Rob and 'Foxy' Tom Dunne, to drive the first wagon; John, 'the older' and Willie 'the lug' Dunne were to take the second, with Joe Telfer and his brother Skinner to steer the third. With the spare horses tied to the wagons, Hinson, Straughen and Badger Weatherburn were to lead the way, leaving Thompson and Hedley from Ellingham at the rear, the pair known to be the finest bowmen in the area.

****

Hinson loved horses. He rode his silver mount at the head of the train from Alnwick with proud satisfaction. It was joked that he would look at a horse first before its rider. How he came to own that silver-coated beauty, five years earlier, was a story often told for amusement.

Riding beyond Whittingham, a hamlet west of Bolton – and where the English army had recently camped before pushing on for Wooler – Hinson had spotted the yearling grazing in a meadow with a string of other horses. Adam Weatherburn and Joe Telfer, who were riding with him, were unable to persuade him to go on until he found out to whom it belonged, and bought it.

It was discovered that the young horse was the property of a small-time merchant who, when approached, immediately declined Hinson's offer, intending to keep the animal for his son. Hinson was desperate and proposed to pay much more than it was worth – twelve shillings, but even this did not sway the merchant's mind. When the three of them rode away, Hinson's face, according to Joe Telfer, was as glum as a toad's.

Next day, Hinson looked pale and unwell; his sleep had been strangled by his failure to purchase the elegant young horse. Badger Weatherburn took him aside. He'd learned that the merchant's abiding interest was horse racing. So strong was his passion, he attended every meeting in the area. Weatherburn proposed that Cuddy Hinson challenge the man, in a bet to win the silver mount. Hinson shook his head, knowing his own pony would be no match for a trained racer.

"Yes," Weatherburn had agreed. "If the race was about speed it wouldn't win, but there's none can match yours for climbing and endurance over rough, moorland ground. You bet him on a hill race instead and you've every chance."

Hinson's face brightened for a moment and then dimmed. "He's not going to be wantin' to race just to keep his own horse, is he?" argued Hinson, his small mouth nipped with doubt.

"No, but we make the bet good enough for him to want to gamble. He needs to be encouraged," quipped Weatherburn with a wily look.

Narrow-eyed, Cuddy Hinson regarded his friend with suspicion, sensing irony. "How?"

"How? How much do you want that horse? That's the question," declared Weatherburn, his brow furrowed.

"What d' you mean?"

"Well if you're really set on havin' it, y'u need to be prepared to make sacrifices for it. Remember it's you that wants a horse that's not for sale."

"Go on," said Hinson, his expression stiff with caution.

Weatherburn spread his arms to show honest reason. "Right, here's an idea. You tell him, if he wins he gets your horse and the twelve shillings, plus the silver one is still his. But if he loses, you still let him have your horse but you get the silver one."

Hinson stared hard at Weatherburn as he pondered the unusual deal. He sniffed and rubbed his chin. Good sense cried "no" but the lovely looking horse ruled his heart. "All right," he said slowly.

That very noon they approached the merchant again and explained the bet and the hill course they had chosen – over the crag at Callaly. The merchant's eyes sparkled at the prospect of easy gain. He had a good fell horse and a rider for it. They shook hands to confirm the deal.

Two days later the race was run with a number of the merchant's friends and associates present. Wearing their red neckerchiefs, Badger Weatherburn and the gang were also there to make certain everything was correct and that the merchant and his cohorts were aware of just who was involved.

Weatherburn's prediction that Hinson's tough little horse would win over hilly ground proved true. He led the race from start to finish, and afterwards the yearling was his to take away. Although the merchant seemed disappointed, he was well compensated by the acquisition of a sturdy, winning mount. Of course, Hinson was jubilant, throwing his arms around his prize's neck, hugging and stroking it; a scene that became etched in the memories of those who'd witnessed the event.

That night at the Coach Inn at Whittingham, Hinson celebrated with his friends and ladies as if he'd won the Crown Jewels. The next day, despite a sore head, he started breaking the animal in, talking and walking it round Beanley Moor.

15

At the Bailiffgate entrance to Alnwick Castle, Heron showed the letter with its seal to the soldiers on guard and they allowed him to enter. At the inner gate he dismounted, leaving a liveryman to lead his horse away for safekeeping, and after a long wait, he was accompanied through an imposing, iron-studded door bearing the Percy Lion crest. Across a courtyard they entered a tower where he was now escorted upstairs by two members of the household guard. He entered a large, wood-panelled hallway leading to a chamber room. Here he was met by Lady Elizabeth Percy, the fifth earl's youngest sister. At the lady's behest, the guards remained stationed outside the door.

In her middle-twenties she was a prim, refined-looking woman, elegantly dressed in a damson-lace costume. Having removed his gauntlets, Heron bowed and presented her with the sealed letter. She opened it carefully, briefly read the message and then placed it on the tasselled, red velvet chair beside her and sat down. She requested that he be seated opposite. An attending servant poured wine for him into a silver goblet and then went to the door. She waited until they were alone, her eyes fixed on Heron as if appraising his appearance against his dubious, amoral reputation.

"It's rare indeed to sit face to face with a noble outlaw," she began, her brow raised and chin lowered discerningly.

"It's rare for me to be one," he answered carefully, with a pinch of humour.

Lady Elizabeth gave a slight, uncertain smile. She had been introduced to him before, incidentally, at a ceremony years previously, and recalled his defensive demeanour, his measured, cagey regard for those outside his immediate circle, and she remembered particularly, as a girl, being warned about him – the fleeting shift of his eyes; the furtiveness of his handsome face; his fierce, lustful temperament.

"We are naturally anxious for William and Lionel, our brothers, in the impending battle against the Scots. And of course, for Henry, our noble earl, fighting in France with our good king. It is reported that the Scottish army is more powerful than the English and that King James is confident of victory. Pray tell me of the situation, John Heron, and I would ask that you speak frankly," she said stiffly, with an air of insistence.

He paused, eyeing her closely and observing that her neck was tinted by a faint flush. Face to face with him, her pertness could not disguise her self-consciousness. Heron considered her slim figure, her long, fair hair and comely face. Despite her frozen look, she was undoubtedly pretty yet still unmarried. It amused him to think of her a virgin and he was fleetingly tempted to try her response to flattery, but thought better of it. He answered her directly.

"You are correctly informed that the Scottish army is larger and that it boasts heavier siege guns, yet that does not mean it is more powerful. Despite his age, the Earl of Surrey has proven himself more competent than King James on the field of battle. I also believe that we Englishmen, in defence of our land, have a stronger reason to achieve victory than do the invaders."

The young Lady Elizabeth Percy stared at him, considering his shrewd reply. "I pray it is so," she answered discreetly. "And what of your position?" she posed.

"My position?" he asked, angling his head to convey surprise.

"Your duty," she answered with hesitation. "Are you simply a messenger?"

He gave a tight-lipped smile. Acting as speaker for the family, she seemed obliged to converse with him, remaining prudent, yet straining to appear composed.

"With respect, my lady, I can say no other," he answered cagily.

"We have already learned of your actions down at the river. Were those your orders?" she challenged him.

Heron confronted her with a roguish gaze. "I do not justify what I have done, only what I will do," he replied artfully.

She smiled – a vague, uncomfortable smile. She clasped her hands together as if in prayer, an act of self-containment. "I understand perfectly," she conceded.

Heron straightened himself in the chair and she saw it as an impatience, a hint that he was ready to go. Lady Elizabeth knew of his former visits to Alnwick and of his interest in the town. She waited for him to finish his drink before she stood, permitting him to take his leave. Courteously, she offered him her hand, which he politely kissed.

"I thank you for your visit and hope that God protects you all. I have a message for you alone to convey to my brothers; say how our love holds with them; that we are proud of their courage and pray for their safety."

Heron noted a change in her voice, a softening, as if she felt some relief that her meeting with him was almost over. He had known from the outset that she was in awe of him.

"Indeed I shall, with pleasure," he answered warmly, giving her some cheer. There was a shade of feeling in her eyes as he turned to depart the tower.

* * * *

Back at the outer gate, he instructed that his horse be left tethered nearby so that next day, before dawn, he would find it, then walked away and into the small town. He moved lightly along a darkening, narrow cobbled street and turned down a damp, guttered side lane, winding towards a row of dim cottages overlooked by the castle's perimeter wall.

Ahead of him, two shabby looking men suddenly emerged from a passageway as he approached, obstructing his pathway. They each held out a hand, a begging gesture, threatening that he should pay in order to pass by. Without the slightest falter in his stride, Heron headed towards them, glaring, and the two vagabonds, sensing his aggression, moved quickly aside before he reached them, and scurried away. Heron continued his walk, his fists uncurling in his gauntlets.

At the end dwelling, he tapped on the door and waited, checking to make sure that he was not being watched. When the door opened slightly, a young woman's face appeared and she quickly took his hand and led him through a narrow entrance into a small, bare, candle-lit room.

Alone, they embraced and kissed with a powerful yearning.

"Aa feared you'd not return," she said, her ebony-coloured eyes gazing up at him. Striking in appearance, her long, loose auburn hair gleamed in the pale, early evening light sifting through the single window.

John Heron pressed his mouth against her cheek. "You fret too much, sweet Ella. I wish to stay and rest here for the night."

She teased him with a smile. "And if Aa say no, will y'u go?"

He shook his head and she gave a short, throaty laugh and squeezed him closer.

The small room was cluttered with a bed and side table, a couple of wooden chairs and a fireplace in which two logs smouldered. A clothes chest sat in a corner. On a broad shelf fixed to the rear wall, an audience of handmade dolls sat, side by side. This was Ella's trade. He'd seen her at a stall the previous summer at Bamburgh Fair and, struck by her sultry, gypsy-like appearance, had made her acquaintance. She had been flattered by the interest from someone of his rank and, disregarding his reputation, was infatuated by the dashing knight, falling headlong in love with him. It was indeed an impossible love and she accepted that it could only exist in seclusion, for his amusement. Yet he treated her with passion and kindness and this was all she, a common girl, could expect.

To make the place more welcoming, she lit two more tallow candles on the table and an oil lamp hanging down from a beam. He stirred the fire, adding a few sticks and balancing some lumps of sea coal upon them. To ensure their privacy she released a blanket, tied above the window, which served as a curtain. A little later while the flames strengthened, she provided him with some bread and sliced pork and a small mug of beer. Afterwards, tipping a jug, she poured some warm water into a bath basin. As he had done on previous visits, Heron quickly stripped off his clothes and standing naked, she gently bathed his face and body. His skin was pale, grimy, stained with sweat, while his physique was honed and sinewy, defined by lean muscles.

Familiar with her touch, he remained unresponsive to her soothing fingers as they talked of various comings and goings in and around Alnwick.

Apart from the few household soldiers that remained at the castle, the earl's retinue had left with him for France while other troops, including tenants from the town, had later followed William and Lionel Percy to strengthen Surrey's army. Ella told Heron how food was becoming scarcer in town owing to short supply and the increased demand by the families massed in the pastures. In turn, she wanted to know of the English army's chances of overcoming the Scottish invaders but John Heron was not inclined to talk of the coming battle and brushed aside any of her questions with facile remarks.

"When I see you again, I'll soak you in the finest of French wines and drink every bit of you."

She regarded him quizzically. "Aa won't thank y'u for it."

He wrapped her tightly in his arms. "Ah, but you will, young Ella, and purr with joy." Kissing her mouth, his hands gripped her hips with sudden desire.

In bed together, naked, their limbs clung in union, striving and heaving, until they were each content and exhausted and their lusts were sated. Afterwards, kissing and caressing, skin damp with perspiration, they lay cheek to cheek, sighing towards a dreamy, sensual sleep. "I love you, Aa do," Ella repeated softly.

His head clouded with fatigue, he merely nudged her in response, for those were words he preserved in memory for his lost, beautiful, and only treasured love.

16

Wednesday night on Flodden Hill. In the air and on the ground, it was a brittle, fitful night. Outside, asleep, soldiers snored and shuffled and fidgeted restlessly in their makeshift beds, and the horses and oxen herded behind the hill snickered and moaned in a disturbed state.

Sounding anxious, owls hooted in relays and the agitated barking of foxes down by the river shrieked up the hillside. In the night sky, a thick slice of moon sidled its way through drab, misty tangles of cloud, scattering shadows like autumn leaves. It had ceased raining, but the soaked earth glistened, like a night of frost.

A restless King James woke with a start at the nibbling sounds of mice. With his mind whirling, he had tumbled into and out of sleep for most of the night. Hastily, rising from his couch, he wrapped himself in a woollen hooded cloak, and stepped into his boots. Calling upon his guards to flush the mice from the room, he made his way outside to be joined by his young, bastard son, Alexander Stewart, Archbishop of St Andrews. Similarly disturbed, he also had wakened and wandered outside his own tent to view the strangeness of the night.

"I see the moon is on its back, which peasant folk consider an ill sign," he muttered pensively, gazing up into the blurred but radiant sky.

King James studied it for a moment, aware of the superstition among his people that he so lamented. "Have no fear of it, Alexander. No doubt it is the same moon that also hangs above the English camp," he reasoned with scorn. "I observe it only as a smile, and an omen for our good." He placed a hand of comfort on his son's shoulder before he moved away, wishing to stand apart, in his own space and thoughts.

Omens irked him. He could not stand to hear of any more. Since his decision to go to war, doom-faced advisers had recounted misfortunes as signs of foreboding. Particularly, a month earlier, when Lord Home's men returning from a retaliatory raid into England, burdened with plunder, were ambushed and scattered near Milfield by a force of archers under Sir William Bulmer, that killed as many as eight hundred and captured the Home Standard. The shadow of this 'Ill Raid', as it was called, was quickly cast over the planned conflict.

But even with inconsequential matters, as when his horse stumbled and he almost fell at the army's mustering point at Ellem Kirk, near Duns, was the incident sewn with prophesy against his invading England and thereby opposing its king, Henry VIII, his own brother-in-law.

Some time later, having returned to his bed, James attempted to relax and fall asleep, but the night air had stimulated him. Wavering in and out of a drowsy stupor, the moon's grin floated through his subconsciousness, fleshing images of familiar faces parading their sceptical, critical gaze at him: the Earl of Angus, Bishop Elphinstone, his queen – Margaret, Bothwell, Crawford, Surrey, Dacre, Lady Heron; mutely, each revealed an ironic, dissident smile before fading away, leaving a solitary figure, head bowed, that he was unable to recognise at first.

Impatiently, he commanded the subject to disclose its identity and as the face slowly lifted, James saw to his great shame and horror, the features of his father, James III, in whose murder he had been complicit, though indirectly in rebellion with others, including the now banished Angus; a murder for which he still endured daily, wearing a chain belt next to his skin as an act of contrition.

Sitting upright with a gasp, fully awake, James wiped the sweat from his brow. With trembling hands flattened tightly together, he uttered a prayer for strength and calm within himself. He declared again his love of God and pleaded for His mercy. Comforted by his faith, he found himself presently released and, within minutes, steadily succumbed into a cradle of exhausted, dreamless sleep.

17

At the first streak of Thursday's dawn entering the room, Heron slid from the bed and dressed hurriedly in the fire's limp glow. Finally, after belting his sword, he placed another log on the embers and then crept to the bed, and bending, kissed her lightly on the brow. She flinched but did not wake. He took some coins from his leather pouch and laid them softly upon the table. Before leaving the room he glanced towards her. She was still asleep.

In the purple light of early morning he made his way back to the castle's outer gate where his horse was tethered and ready for him, as he had requested. Four soldiers on guard watched his every movement as he mounted and rode away. Before sunrise, he had crossed the River Aln and was loping through the woods towards higher ground and dingy, open moorland. Although in haste, Heron viewed with fascination the fronds of amber, yellow light veined between grey and charcoal clouds sprouting in the eastern sky.

Inside an hour and a half he finally reached Wooler Haugh, finding the English camp already crawling with activity. Tatters of river mist and fire smoke were woven like strands of gauze above the dank motion of waking bodies. Throughout the tension of the night, the cooks and their helpers, under orders, had worked ceaselessly, baking and roasting and boiling most everything left in their stores. The soldiers, yawning, bleary-eyed and numb-headed from a nervy, restless sleep, were starting to straggle together in their groups by the fires, waiting for food and direction. Only those too sick to move were left at rest, hunched miserably beneath whatever helped keep them warm, and alive – cloaks, blankets or animal hides.

Spying their leader arriving in camp, Hinson, with his friend from Ewart, Badger Weatherburn, strode over to meet Heron as he slid down from his panting horse. Cuddy Hinson, full of energy as usual, was eager to tell Heron of the greeting they had received when they'd arrived back, yesterday evening, with the loaded wagons. "A crowd o' soldiers followed 's in, happy as hounds at the sight o' food – their eyes on the two deer and three boar lying on top of the pile, which Thompson and Hedley shot on the way back."

Enthusiastically, Hinson went on to say how Lord Dacre, with Bulmer at his side, had expressed delight at their achievement and instructed that the supplies be distributed fairly, even if it meant no more than just an extra mouthful for each soldier. "However," Hinson added, "Dacre twisted his mouth and puffed right annoyed when he heard of y'u staying in Alnwick, leaving us, your men, to return to Wooler without y'u. He called y'u an unfit person, whatever it means," Hinson smirked. He also informed Heron that a cold-faced Sir William Bulmer, upon hearing this too, had simply shaken his head and grunted his disapproval. "He's an odd one," said Hinson. "At least Dacre speaks his mind."

"What did you tell them?" Heron demanded, prickled by the news.

Hinson's small mouth seemed to squeeze out the words. "Dacre wanted t' know where y'u were an' Aa said you'd gone to the Percys' castle with a message. No more than that."

"You didn't mention the girl?" As soon as he had asked this, Heron regretted his words. Lord Dacre, Warden of the West March on the Border was a powerful baron whose influence spread right along the frontier. He and Home, the Scottish lord, were sworn enemies, but also, as politics sometimes proved, were quite capable of collusion if it suited them both. Mindful of his future, John Heron felt it best to forge some kind of accord with Dacre that was lenient. Unwittingly, the advantage he sought had too readily surfaced in his hasty retort.

"Of course Aa didn't. Aa may not be able t' read and write like Weatherburn here, but I'm not stupid," grinned Hinson.

"Only someone stupid would admit it," quipped Adam Weatherburn, who was a bit of a rarity himself, self-educated, witty and ironic.

Unsmiling, John Heron gazed past them at a file of levy soldiers shuffling sullenly towards a feeding post where a chunk of bread and a spoonful of potage was dropped into each man's bowl. "Weatherburn," he said suddenly, without looking at him, "I want you to find William Percy and tell him no more than I carried his letter to the castle and delivered it into his sister Elizabeth's hands."

Weatherburn's brow furrowed. "No more?"

"That's what I said," Heron replied irritably, then turned to Hinson. "You make sure our men are first in line to receive food and drink." He lowered his voice. "Say nothing, both of you, but we'll be moving from here this very day."

Cuddy Hinson nodded. "It's been talked about, Sir, an' the men know fine well. It's there in the air an' in everybody's eyes."

Even though formal instructions had yet to be issued, the English soldiers were secretly aware of the day's importance. After the rustlings of a tremulous night, the morning was suffused with expectation and instincts were primed by a sense of change, a sense of going. Hearts, dragged down by weariness, boredom, hunger and sickness were beginning to pump blood more surely round lethargic limbs. Drained by the sufferance of their abject waiting, the English ranks were desperate for the spark of action that this new day so vibrantly pledged. Consequently, every conversation was riddled with lively speculation, anticipating how the day might unroll.

18

Downstream, in and around the abandoned dwellings of Wooler township burned and ruined by marauding Scots, Stanley's soldiers from Lancashire and Cheshire had set up camp. Two officers, Thomas Venables and Robert Fouleshurst who shared a surviving, empty tavern room, had ridden downhill to ford the small river, known simply as the Wooler Water. On the other side of the stream they were joined by Sir Christopher Savage, commander of a Macclesfield unit. Before going on to take breakfast with other fellow officers, they paused to wonder at the violet-tinged light cascading over the hills from the blurred canopy of the rising sun.

"What an odd but wonderful array of colours this morning brings," remarked Venables, a hearty, red-faced knight with a bass-sounding voice.

"Indeed," exclaimed Sir Christopher. "There is a dreamlike quality to it. A painter's dream." His white horse threw up its head. "See, even my horse is taken with it," he laughed.

"More likely unnerved by it, I'd say," countered Robert Fouleshurst, an elegant, courteous gentleman. "It was an impossible night for sleep."

"It was indeed," agreed Sir Christopher. He raised a hand to stroke his trim, pointed, coppery beard, a look of amusement in his face. "One of my sergeants said he dreamed of the river carrying a swathe of dying fish as gulls swooped over them, pecking their eyes. I praised his description of the hellish scene though he declined the compliment, claiming it was not of his making."

They walked their horses over a stretch of flat ground that was crammed with dreary-faced soldiers and their baggage. Those who had received food ate slowly as if savouring every morsel before swallowing. As the three gentlemen on horseback passed them, unhappy, sullen men glanced up acidly, resentful of their superiors; a silent warning that this lingering and miserable existence was no longer bearable. Venables, Fouleshurst and Savage could feel the sting of their disgruntlement.

At a large pavilion tent they dismounted. They too had yet to receive direct instructions for the day, but expected Surrey's meeting with his military council, due in the hour, to end the speculation that buzzed like flies across the campsite.

"I can understand the men's frustration," said Venables, candidly. "As are we, they're anxious to move from here to confront the enemy. Idleness breeds dissatisfaction. See how aggrieved the men are becoming."

"The question is where? And how?" Fouleshurst rejoined. "I'm loath to own that I'm tired of thinking on't, over and over, contemplating what each day might bring. Surely, there is some purpose in our leaders' silence."

Climbing down from their saddles they handed charge of their horses to a retainer and stepped inside the knights' pavilion, eager to meet other peers and gentry, already gathered there to be served breakfast.

19

In his headquarters, Thomas Howard, Earl of Surrey, his two sons, Thomas the Lord Admiral, and his younger brother, Edmund, were seated at the table. Also seated were Sir Edward Stanley, Sir Marmaduke Constable, Sir William Bulmer and Lord Thomas Dacre. Standing behind them were other leaders under their command: amongst them, from Yorkshire, Lord Latimer, Lord Clifford and Lord Scrope; from Lancashire, Bishop James Stanley, Thomas Strangeways and Sir William Molyneux; from Durham, the Bishop of Durham, Lord Lumley, and Lord Conyers; from Northumberland, William Percy, Robert Ogle, and the Bastard Heron.

Heron's inclusion proved unpopular with the majority of these aristocrats. As a knight his status had been besmirched and overtaken by his notoriety as a criminal outlaw, yet the Earl of Surrey insisted he be present, and the earl's say was final in this case. Lord Dacre had earlier summoned Heron to inform him of Surrey's invitation, although he also expressed his own opposition to it. Furthermore, he upbraided Heron for a breach of duty in failing to return to camp from Alnwick at the head of his troopers. Heron offered no excuse and his only answer was that he'd had other matters to attend to. Dacre's exasperation at Heron's glibness was still evident as the meeting assembled, and he disregarded his presence as though he were a mere lackey.

Surrey began his introduction, speaking with assurance and gravity. "We are all truly mindful of this day's magnitude. The organisation of our march, the aim and purpose of it, requires us to administer and inspire the army we command. Our instruction must be decisive. If there be any inkling of uncertainty or doubt in our authority, the resolve of our men will falter. Therefore I stress that we here, together, be bold in judgement and fearless in our objective to fight and vanquish the invading Scots." His voice grew strident. "As Commander-in-Chief of this army," he declared,

"I have the utmost confidence in you – my leaders, as have I in the momentous task we are about to undertake in the name of England and King Henry." Surrey paused to look round at each individual gathered in the room, personalising his entreaty. "Agreed?" he urged, aloud.

"Agreed!" they chorused, declaring their wholehearted support. Since all had been consulted and involved in planning the encircling march, there was a strong sense of union amongst them. Surrey's drive and care engendered a human link. And he seemed unflappable.

The old earl continued, stressing how King James's refusal to relinquish his position on Flodden Hill had forced their plan. Then he began, with relish, to describe the operation of marching from Wooler Haugh, to cross the River Till by bridge and ford and the route beyond, over Doddington Moor to Barmoor where they would camp that night. Admiral Howard set out the details and order of the procession, instructing those in charge of the various divisions of their duties. He then turned to Heron. "We ask that you give more precise detail of the route, and of the site where we should make camp later in the day. We must leave nothing to chance," he advised.

In his summary, Heron's delivery was direct and assured and his resonant voice gripped the attention of his audience. William Percy of Alnwick, also knowledgeable of the area, raised his hand. "What is the reason, I wonder, for the overnight camp to be fixed a mile beyond Barmoor height, where I believe the ground to be drier for soldiers to lie upon?" His questioning unveiled his superior attitude towards Heron.

Before replying, Heron looked to Surrey to offer the answer, but the old general indicated for Heron to explain, satisfied with the outlaw's composure and manner of dealing with the air of opposition that he faced.

He directed his words firmly towards Percy. "It is a bare moor, hence its name, and our troops would be more exposed to harsh weather. Not only will the lower ground provide better shelter in and about the trees and bushes growing there, but there is also clean spring water." He paused before proceeding. "What's more, the Scots will be of a mind that we are on our way to Berwick. Were we to camp on Barmoor for the night, we would continue to alert them to the possibility of our taking the road to Ford, the following morning, in an attempt to assault their flank. In truth, the longer we hold the enemy in suspense, the more time we have for manoeuvre," he ended solidly, aware that his words had made an impact. Heron supposed, also, engaging Dacre's stare, that he had said enough and not exceeded his role.

"Thank you, John Heron," the admiral said appreciatively. He then resumed to stress the importance of secrecy, and that decisions further than the day ahead would depend on the reaction of King James to the English movement. He raised his chin imperiously and his tone sharpened. "I urgently remind you, honourable leaders, that your troops must know nothing of tomorrow's intent. No one beyond this room must be privy to our plan." He fell silent, briefly, so that his words were framed in their minds. "Now, I desire that each one of us speak with his captains. Together we must ready the men. Once they have eaten a last, prepared meal at midday, we shall set off on the march. I fear," he added grimly, "there will only be scraps left for them to carry on the journey."

Finally, the Earl of Surrey heaved himself onto his feet and, raising a fist in a grand, concluding gesture, he implored them to rally their men with hope and heart, and as he made the sign of the cross upon his chest, to trust in God's good Grace. After a brief prayer led by Bishop James Stanley, the room began to empty. Just as Heron was about to exit, he was abruptly ordered by the earl to stay. Lord Dacre, Admiral Howard and his father, the earl, remained at the table. "Be seated," gestured Surrey, indicating Stanley's vacant chair opposite him. Cagily, Heron obeyed, his dark eyes narrowing, skipping from face to face.

"I shall be blunt," began Surrey when the room was theirs alone. His voice was stern. "Your venture to Alnwick, I believe, was successful. The thieves were punished and the supply wagons brought here to us." Heron sat sullen-faced, blankly expecting a further reprimand for his single dalliance in Alnwick. "We congratulate you for this and, moreover, for the accomplished manner that you addressed the meeting. After a deal of thought and persuasion, I have decided to appoint you second-in-command under Lord Dacre, in charge of the Border cavalry division." Surrey paused to observe Heron's expression, which did not alter. "With some reluctance, Lord Dacre has consented to this proposition. Therefore, vow before me to obey his rule and serve him with due honour. Give me your answer."

Bastard Heron looked at Dacre and the two of them held each other's stare, like crossed swords, neither wanting to give way.

"Yes or no?" repeated Surrey, impatiently.

"Yes," affirmed Heron.

With the suggestion of a smile, Dacre leaned slightly towards him. "Despite my reservations, it is apparent that our Border men already consider you as a talisman and their champion. Your reiver exploits of daring and cunning excite the common people. I expect you, John Heron of Ford, to be my champion too. Whatever your man, Hinson, means to you, I want you to mean the same to me. Do you understand?"

Heron's eyes opened wider, causing him to frown. The trust bequeathed in him by these three men filled his chest like a clean breath of air. He had no words to speak of his feeling. He merely nodded his head slowly in acceptance.

Lord Dacre was insistent. "I want a reply I can hear. Are you prepared to follow me as faithfully as he follows you?"

Heron allowed the edge of a smile to lighten his seriousness. "Hinson follows me like a lion, not a dog. I'll do the same for you, my Lord Dacre."

Surrey chuckled. "As long as you don't maul him, Heron, I think we can accept that. But remember," he cautioned, his eyes firming, "you are not yet pardoned, so the noose for your neck has not been cut down."

Dacre and the admiral were amused at the earl's comment; how often he applied witticism in his censure of others in place of bare threat. While they chortled, Surrey and Heron smiled stealthily at each other. Heron was aware that the old earl had favoured him, and permitted him – the miscreant, the outlaw, the outsider – into his inner council. Yet his remark, flippant as it seemed, was no joke but a signal of power, like the fist he'd raised earlier before everyone; a signal that he would not tolerate any failing or misdemeanour in Heron that would offend or injure his divisional leader, and friend, Lord Thomas Dacre of Gilsland.

20

Horns blasted and orders were bawled throughout the ranks. At once, a great physical and mental jolt shook off the burden of suspension that clung to the men. Set free from indecision, an exhilaration stampeded over the camping ground with a clatter and clamour as everyone moved purposely, in readiness for the push. Although a few individuals showed open delight at the move, the rest were rock-faced as they prepared, keeping in check any feelings of nervousness or suspicion.

Under the surveillance of Nicholas Appleyard, the artillery guns were hauled into position and fastened to teams of horses already harnessed. Since England's heaviest artillery accompanied King Henry's army in France, Appleyard's twenty-three pieces – five brass serpentines and eighteen falcons – were lightweight compared to the Scottish cannon though easier to handle.

Elsewhere, the foot soldiers, mainly bill-men and bowmen from the feudal estates plus a sizeable number of professional men-at-arms, busied themselves with their armour and weapons, which would be carried to battle. The cavalry, mostly Border lancers, or 'prickers' as they were commonly known, were dressed in their traditional steel bonnet helmets and light, leather, metal-plated jackets over their shirts. Long, thick leather riding boots covered their britches. Gathering their lances, swords, small bows and saddles, they were eager to mount up and ride out under Lord Dacre, with Bastard Heron, his newly appointed second-in-command, alongside him at the fore. Once again, Heron remained distinctive in his black garb and red cape whilst his followers were identifiable by the red kerchiefs fastened round their necks. The rest of the cavalry, roughly seventeen hundred of them, wore white armbands. Sensibly, Dacre had no objection to this discrimination, appreciating the dread that would fume through the Scottish Borderers at the sight of Heron's savages.

Despite the English army's desire to set out at once, the signal to leave was delayed until the soldiers had eaten the little there was left. Then they were swiftly mobilised by mounted knights and captains into unit formations identified by their badges, bands and uniforms, over which the standard, sleeveless white over-vest with its red cross was worn. Finally, at the sound of horns blaring and orders bellowing, the long march began in weak sunlight through a lead-dull, misty drizzle.

The main vanguard accompanying the artillery was led by the Lord Admiral, Thomas Howard, while its two wing sections went together with their leaders, Sir Marmaduke Constable and Edmund Howard. Following them came the main rearguard division under the Earl of Surrey and its two wings led by Sir Edward Stanley and Lord Thomas Dacre. Held proudly erect at the head of the initial separate routes, the king's Royal Standard led the way towards the bridge at Weetwood while the banner of Saint Cuthbert, with Sir William Bulmer and Lord Lumley of Durham, moved off downstream towards the ford crossing – the holy flag, an emblem of heaven, pointing the way; either way, to live or die. Also, down the columns of soldiers, the heavy array of other banners and flags swayed limply in the sombre, damp air.

Watching them depart, camp followers stood with hearts stretched by both pride and anxiety. For the women who saw their menfolk disappearing into the distance, feelings were frayed as they suppressed their inner fears. Finally, turning away to begin the enormous, filthy task of clearing the ground, stained by the mess and rubbish left behind by the thousands, they could only reflect upon the comfort they gave to lighten the hardship and misery of their dear ones' stay.

Only soldiers that were severely ill were permitted to remain behind and, glancing at one such fellow coughing and retching where he lay huddled, Jenny Charlton, Seth's sister, almost wished it were Mossy, her husband and father to a first child she could feel within her. Here, at least his fate would have rested with her and not with the cruel, careless blade of the feared enemy.

21

Behind the English king's Royal Standard, directed by the admiral, the main vanguard's column made slow but dry progress across the narrow, arched bridge at Weetwood, after which they rounded the hill ahead of them along a rain-splattered, sandy track. Meanwhile its wing divisions had to contend with the swollen river at the ford downstream, the flood caused by almost three weeks of constant, sweeping rain. Following the vanguard, the rearguard under Surrey was likewise divided in order to traverse the River Till at both crossings. To assist the infantry over the ford, Lord Dacre deployed his cavalry to ferry vital equipment and baggage, and to support the wading soldiers who, arms linked, splashed through the water rushing above their knees and tugging at their legs.

It was not without amusement. A couple of levy soldiers from Lancaster, stubbornly refusing assistance, lost their footing and toppled from the shallows into the deeper current, sailing off downstream, crying for help. Two horsemen pounded along the bank and, crashing into the river, dragged them out like dripping cats. Returned to their comrades, they were loudly mocked for their stupidity and, without pity, the two marched on in silence, wet, humbled and ridiculed.

Beyond the Till, nearing Doddington, both routes merged into one and the flag-emblazoned line of over twenty-two thousand men slowly trailed through the burnt-out hamlet, previously ruined by marauding Scots, and ascended a long slope, moving northwards onto Doddington North Moor. To guard the march, Lord Dacre sent Heron with forty of his two hundred riders to the west of the line, to check on the Scottish position and to scare or even capture any spies that chanced too near.

Given this assignment, Bastard Heron followed his own instincts, calling on a patrol of twenty experienced fighters and bowmen, led by Cuddy Hinson, to probe the lower woodland closer to the Till, sniping at any of the enemy they spotted.

Surrounded by mounted men-at-arms, a pensive Surrey sat robed in his horse-drawn carriage. Brow lowered, he surveyed the vanguard's column of troops stretching in front of him over the skyline. He envisaged how King James would receive news of the English army marching north on the other side of the river from Flodden. Surrey knew James personally, having been in his company a number of times, particularly during negotiations for the 'Treaty of Perpetual Peace' in 1502, and then the following year at the celebrations of James's marriage to the fourteen-year-old princess, Margaret Tudor. Indeed, they were seen together there as friends. So now, in this respect, he could well picture James's aloof expression, the tightening of his mouth to hide his puzzlement, or his short, hollow laugh at the possibility of the English army, enfeebled by hunger, illness and desertion, backing away from the fight to seek respite in Berwick. No matter how James reacted, Surrey was sure of one thing: the king would do only what he chose or wished, paying little or no attention to others' suggestions, regardless of delay. In plotting this march, Surrey relied heavily upon this trait and willed it with all his heart.

Rocking in his carriage seat, his reverie was wiped out by the distant booms of gunfire and the crash of cannon balls smashing into the wood, half a mile to the east of them. In camp at Wooler they had heard shots in the distance as the Scottish crews on Flodden, six miles away, practised for range, but now their destruction was nearer, the impact sounded more real and frightening. Ducking in fear, many of the foot soldiers in the line cowered, unnerved by the thunderous din, the like of which they'd never encountered before. One soldier, losing his nerve, made a frantic dash through the bracken to escape. A sergeant on horseback gave chase and, grabbing him by the collar, hauled him back to join the halted column. Seeing the incident up ahead, Surrey ordered that the fugitive be brought to him at once.

Panic-bitten, the struggling soldier was still in a state of shock, whimpering as he arrived at Surrey's carriage. His captor thrust him nearer. Surrey leaned closer to the man's tearful, grimaced face. "Be silent," he rasped. Confronted by the general's close scowl, the wretch ceased to babble, his lips twitching. "Tell me your name," Surrey demanded.

"Sn-itch! Edward Snitch," he blurted out. Although his face was that of a young man's, his wispy beard showed streaks of grey. His cheeks were drawn and pale, caused by the sickness that had infected so many. He was wearing a steel cap and under the white sleeveless surcoat, a padded jerkin with an orange-coloured band sewn round his left arm, this identifying him as a soldier from Yorkshire's East Riding.

Surrey understood the man's anguish. "Edward Snitch, aye? A fine family name from Hull, or thereabouts."

The man stared, red eyed, blinking. "From Sculcoates, Sir," he mumbled.

Surrey smiled slightly, holding the other's attention. "Listen to me, Edward. We're beyond reach of those guns and none can harm us. I want you to go back to your place and march on. I want you to prove to your family that you have courage, that you have loyalty, and that you are proud to fight for your king and country. I want you, Edward, to fight for all those back home in Sculcoates, for all those who know you, and for me too, Edward." His tone crisped. "Men like you can win the battle. Your determination and striving can bring us victory, defeating the invaders. Turn your fear into strength. Hurl away the dread that shrivels your heart and feed it instead with courage. Remember your name, Edward Snitch. Remember it and honour it like a crown. Wear it with valour," he appealed with passion.

Edward Snitch gaped, absorbed by the words. He heaved a breath and then, mouth clenched shut, turned and walked away, unescorted, back to his place. Surrey said no more, leaned backwards into his seat and signalled by hand for the section to continue its march.

22

Early Thursday afternoon, on Flodden Hill riders galloped through the Scottish ranks delivering messages to the divisional commanders and officers. The news exploded. The English were marching north, away from the wide Till Valley that ran towards the Scottish position upon the hill beyond Milfield. There was an immediate slap of surprise and suspicion. What was their destination? Berwick? Norham? Scotland? With time to reflect upon it, confusion gave way to an air of jubilation. Surrey's army was on the road to Berwick. The English did not want to fight. But why? What was their objective? Would they restock supplies and prepare for an invasion? Still, whatever their motive, its outcome lay in the future. For now, the battle seemed to be suspended. And by failing in their commitment to it, the English were, it appeared, admitting defeat. After tomorrow, Friday 9th September, the Scottish army would have the privilege of retiring homeward in triumph, without engagement. And ideally, Scotland's obligation to show its support of the French, by stepping into England, would be fulfilled.

Despite this growing optimism, a core of the nobility still felt a nip of distrust. King James had ordered Borthwick's cannon to fire a salvo towards Doddington, which some saw merely as a vain act of supremacy, or disdain. Those senior earls and lords who'd had dealings with Surrey in the past and thus were familiar with his tenacity and scheming, could not believe he would simply concede. He was not that sort of general, not that kind of man. Nevertheless, the reality was there to consider. Advancing northwards, the English were steadily moving away from Flodden and the conflict appeared unlikely. Yet, to his credit, until his spies confirmed it, King James ordered his army to hold its position and stand firm.

At their campsites, the common Scottish soldiers had heard the news and throngs of men celebrated with song and dance. But then, learning that they had to remain another day, groans of disappointment were uttered, especially from those who lived in the northern parts of Scotland, and thus with further to return home. After all, the campaign was dragging towards the end of their forty-day period of feudal service. And with the English army on the retreat, it seemed futile remaining any longer on English soil when their country – their homeland – lay invitingly, a mere four miles or so to the northwest of them, beyond the River Tweed.

The Teviotdale contingent, having returned from afternoon drill with their French instructors in use of the eighteen-foot pike, gathered round fires to toast dough and swig a measure of ale. Home for many of them was no more than a day's ride so their thoughts were less emotive. If the enemy had left their camp and tomorrow came and went without a fight, another night on the hill made no difference. They could be home the following day.

Jock Burn and Tickler Tait stood together, entertained by the action of a small football game. Jock's four sons with two older cousins made up a team against another six, all Taits, relatives from another branch of Tickler's family. It was good-natured but the cloth-stuffed, flimsy ball was played more by luck than skill, while the slope of the hill and the muddy ground added greatly to the excitement and humour of the game. The age of Jock's sons ranged from young Ewan who was thirteen years old, to Dody who was twenty, and they were robust country lads. Challenges and tackles were physical and clumsy, encouraged by raucous spectators ringed around the small pitch.

"Your boys aren't feared o' the bigger men," admitted Tickler Tait with a grin.

"They're used t' scrappin' wi' each other. An' Dody, Wullie an' Tucker are top wrestlers at the Fairs," said Jock, keeping his eyes on the game.

Playing goal stopper, young Ewan Burn chose rashly to run out and kick the ball, and slipping, miss-hit it to an opponent. With Ewan on his backside, out of position, it was a great opportunity for the other to score. Taking aim he swung his foot and as the ball looped towards the open goal, Ewan somehow managed to scramble onto his feet, race back and hurl himself into the air to push the ball wide. The incredible save stunned all who saw it into a moment of silent wonder, before they jumped up and down and howled in sheer delight. Surrounded by players from both sides, young Ewan, beaming, was patted like a winning pony.

"If Aa hadn't seen it wi' m' own eyes Aa wouldn't have believed it," confessed Tickler, shaking his head in amazement.

"Me neither," said Jock proudly, still taking it in.

The game continued, but the daring save seemed to incite the players to show more verve and grit. Before very long, the rough and tumble became noticeably more reckless. Also, the previous humour and friendliness seemed to disappear as brawn and aggression took over. Bodies flew in, fouls increased and tempers were rising.

"Someone's ganna get hurt," Jock muttered.

He had hardly said these words when Tucker and one of the opposition charged towards a loose ball and slid in, feet first, colliding heavily, with the crack of breaking bone distinctly heard. The game came to a halt. The older player, a Tait, rose to his feet and hobbled in pain, while sixteen-year-old Tucker Burn remained on the ground, writhing in agony, clutching his leg. Jock and other spectators rushed to him. Among the crowd, accusations and insults were mouthed and angry punches were thrown before the troublemakers could be pulled apart and calm was restored.

Tucker's lower leg was misshapen. In torment, he held his head in his hands. A wooden pallet was quickly fetched and he was carefully rolled onto it, and his father and five other men transported him gingerly to a monks' tent for treatment.

The two monks from Soutra, near Edinburgh, skilled in dealing with ailments and injuries, gave the lad a potion to drink in order to drowse and relax him. Soon afterwards, with his father and another man holding him down, the two monks manipulated the leg as straight as they could and bound it with bandages to a wooden splint. Despite the drug, the boy's cries of pain were clearly heard by the large family crowd gathered outside. When the treatment was completed, it was decided that Jock would stay beside his anguished son through the coming night. The next day, Friday, the monks would assess the patient's condition, and dependent upon the day's circumstances, decide for the lad to be transported to the Priory's hospital in Coldstream or, perhaps, all the way back home to Langholm.

23

King James rode proudly amongst the divisions of his army, meeting his leaders informally. Morale was high. Optimism abounded. In many sections he was not only saluted but also cheered. He felt this adulation like a reprieve, a vindication of his zeal and, moreover, his pledge to honour Scotland's long-standing alliance with France; it seemed that his kingship and valour had been endorsed by the voice of his people. Adding to this, he had received confirmation of his letter reaching Lady Heron in Berwick. Her opal brooch nestled inside a pocket beneath his mail jacket. His heart beat lightly, fanned by elation and a sense of destiny – a king, supreme.

By the time he returned to his royal pavilion, late afternoon, he was enthralled by the latest report of Surrey's movement approaching Barmoor. His spies had encountered resistance, three or four of them presumed killed by English bowmen and one believed to have been captured alive. But a band of Scottish raiders had ambushed two of Heron's men, one of them a vital henchman called Hinson, and cut both down.

King James dismissed the messenger and then turned to his son, Alexander, Stuart, Archbishop of St Andrews, and to his friend, Adam Hepburn, Earl of Bothwell. "It wearies me greatly to hear again and again of the outlaw Heron. I shall rejoice the day someone throws his head down at my feet."

"He is but a rogue knight and not worthy of your attention, my king," replied Bothwell.

"I agree," said the Archbishop. A tall, handsome young man,

ostentatious like his father, he continued, "The Kers will hunt him down one day, that is certain. The adversary we should consider most is not Heron, but the Earl of Surrey. So far his intentions are unclear. Presently his army appears to be heading for the safety of Berwick. But is it? What's in his mind?"

King James gave him a knowing stare. "Surrey has his two sons with him. Militarily, the youngest, Edmund, is raw and inexperienced. His older brother, the admiral, despite his threats and bluster, is a mere soldier of the sea. I doubt Surrey will risk members of his own family without any reasonable chance of victory. Remember, he has already lost a son, Edward, at sea, attacking the French. Unless I am mistaken, the English army is marching north to avoid the shame of heading south. It's Surrey's artful way of retreating with a mask of honour. I know the man from personal experience. I even, dare I say, liked him. But his army is no match for ours and he comprehends it," King James asserted with pride, a trace of a smile puckering the corners of his mouth.

Enlivened by the day's turn of events, the king called out, ordering a servant to pour three goblets of wine. They were seated comfortably when another messenger entered with surprising but favourable news that the Earl of Caithness was approaching camp bringing an additional three hundred soldiers. The earl, who had been in dispute with his king, had relented at this late stage and sought to join the Scottish army. James rejoiced instantly at the news, seeing it as further confirmation of his position and good fortune. A look of complacency flickered in his eyes. "It pleases me that there is much for which to be grateful. I desire that the earl be escorted to join me as soon as he arrives at Flodden."

In order that the reunion with Caithness be celebrated fittingly, King James asked for other leading commanders to be invited to the meeting. Promptly summoned, it wasn't very long before his senior nobles, Home, Huntly, Errol, Crawford, Montrose, Lennox and Argyll, joined His Majesty, His Grace the Archbishop, and the Earl of Boswell, and more wine was poured.

Lord Home, whose scouts had been tracking Surrey's march

throughout the afternoon, delivered the latest information – that the English were about to camp overnight just to the north of Barmoor Tower, near the hamlet of Bowsden. No one was startled by this proceeding. Although their journey from Wooler was relatively short, the organisation of a camp on this scale required enough daylight for it to be achieved. It also indicated the fatigue and condition of their troops, hard pressed by previous marching over many, many days.

A map was rolled out once again to illustrate the route the English had taken and where their camp was located, roughly eight miles south of Berwick and seven miles north-east of Flodden. "Reliable accounts estimate their army to be a third fewer than ours," added Home, the Border lord. Still smarting from defeat and the loss of the Home banner near Milfield, in early August, at the hands of Bulmer's English archers, Alexander, Lord Home remained suspicious of Surrey's withdrawal. His eyebrows arched. "I do not understand what advantage he seeks moving his army northwards. If they advance towards us through Ford, our guns will destroy them before they cross the Till. The only other option is for them to circle round from the north, but that would be extreme, even madness." Home threw up his arms to underline his wonderment.

King James snorted. "Do not be perplexed, my Lord Home. Surrey would not be so foolish as to risk defeat at the unlikelihood of victory. Whatever he does, however he tries, we shall not be knocked off this hill." Reading the satisfaction his words evoked in the minds of his glowing audience, he raised his goblet to toast their homage to him. "To you, my noble commanders; I esteem your courage and your faithfulness." He sipped his wine, then uplifted by the blessings of the passing day – the possibility of Surrey's removal, Lady Heron's brooch, the imminent arrival of Caithness with more fighting men, and the veneration of his soldiers as he passed by – he asked everyone to raise their goblets with his. "To Scotland, to the bravery of its soldiers and, yes, to tomorrow. Tomorrow!" he repeated loudly.

"Tomorrow!" they responded jubilantly and let the drain of fine wine flush inside their mouths before they swallowed.

* * * *

Earlier that same afternoon, on the other side of the River Till, within shouting distance of one another, the four Dunne brothers, Thompson and Hedley quietly searched the woods on horseback. Their faces were sombre. They had been the last to see Hinson and Joe Telfer. When the two of them failed to return to the arranged meeting spot, at the time when the pale afternoon sun was half lowered, the others sensed misfortune.

Seeing a trail of bent, broken bracken, Hedley and Thompson followed it down to a bank where a stream bubbled into a small glade. There, tied at their ankles, the two stripped, mutilated bodies were hanging upside down, like plucked chickens, from a birch tree's branch. The two riders paused to scan the area before Hedley whistled, imitating a lapwing's call, to attract the others.

Once they had gathered, their faces scored by shock and rage, the group cut the ropes and laid the bodies of their friends down. No words were uttered, the six of them dismayed and angry at the mistake of it. Hinson and Telfer had survived countless fights and skirmishes and had ended up carelessly isolated, trapped and murdered by Kers who had left their customary trademark, the spearing of eyes. Wrapping each body in cloaks, they tied them across a single mount and set off to face Heron with the awful news.

24

When he learned of the deaths of Cuddy Hinson and Joe Telfer, John Heron's eyes seemed to freeze. Having known them since boyhood when he'd taught them to sword-fight, he now felt their loss bitterly and his gaze dropped to the ground. Leaden-faced, he pondered, grieved and baffled as to how a man like Hinson, completely alert to danger, could be taken. Hinson, three months older than Heron, had been his hired servant and guard since he, a young knight, had reached manhood. In due course, Hinson had proven invaluable as a protector, ally and aide. His cheerfulness and vitality, linked to fierce courage, was irreplaceable. Joe Telfer, quiet and tough, had been a leading figure in the raiding parties since they began and, remarkably, he had never been wounded in the least way.

Heron raised his eyes skywards, heaved a sigh and walked to the horse bearing the two slumped bodies tied across the saddle. While his men watched, he himself cut the cords, lowered them to the ground and uncovered them. Stripped of helmets, jerkins, boots and weapons, their naked bodies revealed numerous spear and sword wounds to body and head.

"Bring me the prisoner," ordered Heron.

The puny, wizened-faced Scotsman, arms bound, was thrust forward. A large growth bulged on his right cheek close to his ear. He trembled with fear. Heron placed his dagger's point against the man's chest, prepared to thrust.

"Who were the riders down by the river?" he demanded fiercely.

The man shook his head. "The' weren't wi' us, I promise," he stammered. Heron waited, his stare stabbing further terror into the prisoner's heart. "We were sent t' watch, not kill," he blurted out.

"Kers?" quizzed Heron.

"Aa think maybe. An' Archie Tait," he added. "Aa heard Archie bragging the' were coming later, after we were gone. There was an Englishman wi' them as well. One o' the Halls, who crossed sides."

Heron lowered his sword for he believed the grubby little man. He could tell that he wasn't lying. Fear couldn't cloud his honest, gentle self. There wasn't a fibre of soldier in him. Heron pointed an accusing finger and demanded to know why he had become a spy.

"Aa wanted to mind after m' young brother that was sent." His tone cracked with grief. "But he got killed by a' arrow."

"Tell me your name."

"Donald Fernie," he replied meekly.

Heron's tone softened. "Where are you from?"

"Haddington."

Heron paused, contemplating the wretch, then astonished those with him by instructing that the prisoner be cut loose and that he, a simple, poor man, could go unharmed, to bury his brother. Heron's mood-shift was typical of him. In a second he could alter from placid to stormy, from violent to reasonable. His men had learned to cope, wary of his temper, keeping an amiable, respectful distance in or outside his company.

Containing his feelings, the Scotsman, with a look of bewilderment, rubbed his wrists and then turned slowly and wandered off – a scrawny, pathetic, lonely figure, trudging through the bracken towards the trees hedging the moor.

Heron and his band remained a while longer to bury Hinson and Telfer with prayer and solemnity. It was a rough, shallow grave, blessed by a loosely made cross of sticks; a place they could locate in days' time to recover the bodies and bury them properly. Adam Weatherburn said a few words in praise of their dead comrades' qualities, hailing them as brave warriors and true men, and so consoling Telfer's brother, Skinner, who shed tears. Meeting no one's eyes, John Heron said nothing. Afterwards, astride their saddles, they rode off bunched together, fronted by Heron with Straughen and Weatherburn at his side, to catch up with the English troops ahead, marching north on the mud-festered road over Barmoor.

25

Around a huge blazing fire, its sparks spouting into the air, those Kers who had been on the foray were cackling, triumphing in the murder of Hinson. Archie Tait, laughing shrilly, held up Hinson's leather-handled sword, which he had claimed before any other, and swung it round his head in a display of merited ownership. "We may not have got Heron but w' have his shadow!" he sang in delight, his blue-green eyes shining like jewels.

Adam Hall, the traitor, sporting Hinson's bone-handled dagger, thrust it aloft in jubilation. An uncouth looking man with a broad scar running down his left cheek, he was boastful of his role. "Like swine to the slaughter pen!" he whooped drunkenly. It was his deception that led Hinson and Telfer to chase after him and into the trap where they were set upon. Hall had wanted one of the two horses, the silver one, but the tall 'Stoopback' Ker and his brother Angus claimed them and no one argued with these two cruel individuals. When Hinson and Telfer lay on their backs, dying, it was these two who finished them off, ramming their lances through their glazed eyes; a ritual they had performed many times.

'Wattie' Ker, a senior member of the Kers of Ferniehurst, approached the group on horseback. Remaining in the saddle, he offered his praise. "We are rightly joyful for what you have accomplished. My family is sworn to kill Heron for the murder of our chieftain, Sir Robert. Your execution of Hinson and Telfer will cause him great anguish. In appreciation of your worthy action and bravery," Wattie proclaimed, "Sir Andrew Ker himself wishes to extend his gratitude." Whereupon Wattie, a pouch full of coins in his left hand, tossed it onto the ground before them, then turned and rode away, leaving the gang of desperates to distribute the money amongst themselves.

A cautious, celebratory mood flowed throughout the Scottish camp. Word had darted gaily across the hill that the English were passing beyond the road to Ford. This seemed to confirm that Surrey was unlikely to mount a possible flank attack but had instead decided to retire to Berwick, as the Scots hoped. Whatever Surrey planned from there on, reinforcing the town or relieving his army, the battle at Flodden appeared no longer imminent, and the bulk of King James's troops – ordinary, common men – anticipated an early release the following day, when their divisions could be disbanded.

26

After Donald Fernie had buried his brother in the wood near Fenton Hill he sat on the ground and sobbed. He found it impossible to reconcile himself to his loss. Astonishingly, he had not been hanged for a spy as he'd expected and was amazed to have been set free, though he hardly cared any more for, inwardly, his brother's death had all but destroyed him. They had always been warm-hearted towards each other, despite the six years between them during which their mother had borne three daughters. As the only other son, he had always acted responsibly, regarding his popular young brother with attention and affection, and never once inflicting hurt or his envy upon him.

Later, when he carefully splashed across the River Till alone, near Milfield, he trudged downstream between the bushes and trees that sprouted thickly over the low ground. Glimpsing Flodden Hill to his left, he crossed the plain and plodded his way up through the mud trampled between the tents and shelters of the camp, to return to his unit. Believed captured or dead, he was greeted with astonishment and interest. Choosing not to mention his encounter with Heron and of his reprieve, he explained sullenly how, in the attack, he had run off to hide until the English riders had gone. He told them he knew nothing of his brother or the others, but feared they were dead, then fell silent.

Left to himself, he gathered and tied his belongings into a bundle then sat alone and waited gloomily, with an empty heart, for dusk to fall. He had never wanted to fight in the first place and, now his brother was gone, there was no reason for him to stay. Suspecting the crossing at Coldstream to be guarded by soldiers charged with obstructing and turning back deserters from the Scottish camp, Fernie intended, in the dim light of evening, to sneak off back to the Till so he could follow it down to where it joined the River Tweed at Tillmouth. Regardless of the risk, and depending on the light of the moon, he hoped to wade across the Tweed into Scotland before midnight.

Donald Fernie was not to know that the river's strong current would sweep him off his feet and that his drowned body would be found the next day, snagged to a dipping branch at the river's edge near Norham, his small trespass into England having ended in full circle.

27

Under the dismal, damp sky of late Thursday afternoon, Lord Admiral Howard led his vanguard troops over the final rise of north Barmoor onto the lower, sparsely wooded broad shelf of ground, located by Heron for camping overnight. Within the hour, Surrey's rearguard divisions arrived to join them. The long, inclined slog had sapped the exhilaration that had roused the troops' conviction and energy when they'd set out from Wooler.

Now, slow moving, the dank-smelling men herded into place like docile cattle and prepared to bed down. Fires were lighted though more for comfort than cooking as there was scarcely a bite left. Even more depressing for them was the desperate shortage of beer and the necessity to drink spring water instead. Yet remarkably, despite their woes, an air of perseverance was sustained amongst the troops, due largely to the optimism displayed by their leaders. The ranks knew nothing of tomorrow but sensed the night would be the last of its kind, bringing to an end the hardship and deprivation that they had doggedly endured, day after day, for nearly two weeks – and for some, even longer.

Barmoor Tower, a minor bastion the Scots had assaulted and despoiled, had been recovered two days earlier by its owner, Muschamp, and was now back in English hands. It was in due course offered to Surrey and his leading commanders as their place of residence and battle headquarters. Before any formal meeting was conducted, the old earl instructed his two sons, with Heron acting as guide and protector, to ride onto Watchlaw Hill where they might possibly observe whether there had been any Scottish movement in reaction to the English march.

Aware of the English party's approach, a team of Scottish spies had already scattered from the hill by the time they arrived. And so, after a brief climb, ringed by reiver men and household guards, the two Howards and Bastard Heron rode across the wide, desolate top of Watchlaw to survey the valley and hills before them.

Even though the light was dull about them, a sheen of sunlight emerging between rain clouds granted them an outstanding view of Flodden Hill to the south-west of their position. Standing upright in his saddle, as if it would give him some advantage, Thomas, Lord Admiral could make out the Scottish encampment and the massed, smoky evidence of its army, still in place. Beside him, his brother Edmund and John Heron remained seated and discerned the situation for themselves: that the Scottish army appeared to have made no move, nor preparation to do so.

The admiral, small, stockily built with a determined, unremitting look, turned his head and lowered himself back onto his saddle. "King James waits, not knowing," he said, intoning his satisfaction.

"Tell us more, brother," Edmund rejoined. Though physically alike, Edmund's manner was less severe and certainly more casual than that of his brother.

"He waits for us because he is uncertain. Not knowing our next move, he holds his ground," the admiral maintained, unable to conceal a touch of impatience.

"Now that I can see the hill, perhaps we ought have launched an artillery attack from this side?" Edmund countered, blandly.

"It was considered, remember? Yet it would be of no avail to launch an attack that we are bound to lose," Thomas replied curtly, irritated by his brother's rash suggestion.

Heron thought it sounded like a reproof, but Edmund took it lightly with a smile. Heron had already perceived a rivalry between them. He'd learned from others that a brother, Edward, killed at sea, had outshone

Thomas and this had marred his relationship with his younger brother, Edmund, who resembled Edward in humour and vitality. The admiral's apparent disdain towards his younger brother reminded Heron of the antipathy he, too, had felt from his older half-brother, William, who'd berated him throughout his boyhood. He remembered, too, that it was this abuse that had encouraged some of the other, older boys, sons of wealthy fathers, also to treat him with contempt.

"What is your say, Heron?" asked the admiral, wisely evading his brother's opinion.

"I agree, my lord. Our only sure way of attack lies from behind the enemy, as we have already agreed, from Branxton Hill, which we can just make out, there." He pointed to the right, towards a ridge beyond Flodden. "Of course, we cannot know for certain that the Scots will stay on Flodden while we move towards them. That's the risk we take," he said plainly.

"Do you mean the risk that they might have gone before we reach them?" chirped Edmund. "Or do you mean that they'll be ready and waiting?"

Heron allowed the trace of a smile. He felt Edmund was being frivolous on purpose, to further aggravate his elder brother. "Who knows?" he replied.

Ignoring an argument that had already been fully debated to a conclusion, Thomas Howard switched from the topic, asking Heron to identify other landmarks so that he might be aware of the local terrain and its geography. As Heron guided his gaze, the admiral digested the information with acute concentration and the astuteness of a natural leader. Like his father, the earl, he possessed a self-conviction that inhabited a stony, attentive silence.

After a long, deliberate stare towards the Scottish camp, Thomas Howard turned his horse and forging well ahead, led the party back across the raised ground down towards Barmoor Wood. Riding side by side, Edmund and John Heron were aware of the responsibility which set the admiral apart from them and understood his need to ride on alone, to contemplate the scene of the following day's action.

"I believe you lost two good men on the way to Barmoor," Edmund said suddenly, raising his voice above the clatter of horses' hooves.

Heron glanced at him. "We did," he replied.

"Do you consider death?" Edmund found himself saying. "I mean your own death?"

Heron looked sternly ahead. "I do not consider it. To do so is foolish."

Edmund was unable to read Heron's reluctance to speak of it. He persevered. "In battle there is every chance of dying. No one can ignore the possibility."

Heron snorted at the young Howard's persistence. He turned to look at Edmund and wondered if it was this doggedness, this tenacity, that his father, Surrey, entrusted in him, as a leader.

"I do not speak of my death, nor entertain the notion," Heron said, choosing a salutary tone. "I see no reason to think of it, and my aim is to make life as difficult for it to occur as I can."

Edmund Howard paused, then laughed aloud. "You jest with me, I think. You have an uncanny twist on words."

John Heron failed to smile. Instead, he brusquely spurred his horse ahead, in order to leave Edmund behind and catch up with the admiral.

Before they reached the tower, the moderate south wind changed direction, strengthening more coldly from the direction of the coast which lay five or six miles to the east of Barmoor. Darker, thicker clouds emerged rapidly and rain began to pummel the ground. Disconsolately, English soldiers quickly hunkered down in what shelter they had or could find, their unease completed by fading daylight, hunger and the thorns of uncertainty.

****

In the lee of a clump of broom bushes, Seth Milburn tightened his tattered sheepskin cloak about his frame. With him, other members of his family and some Charltons were similarly wrapped against the blustery splash. They were chewing pork rinds that Little Lance Milburn had bargained from some Yorkshiremen on the march.

"How much did y'u pay them?" asked Seth, chewing.

"More than their worth," muttered Lance, eluding the question.

Seth's grin covered his face. "It's not that A'm nosy. I wanted to give y'u something towards whatever the' cost, that's all."

His uncle shrugged away the offer and continued munching, sucking all the goodness he could extract from the strip of burned flesh.

Even for tough, hardy frontier men such as these, living through the past week of squalor, sickness and short supplies had been dreadful. "Hell can't be worse than this," groaned Mossy Charlton.

"Hell's got to be warmer," declared Lance with dry humour. His tongue came out to curl round his mouth, licking up any grease he had missed. "An' Aa wish t' hell w' knew what we're doing, an' where we're goin'," he muttered impatiently. "A'm losin' belief in what we're here for in the first place."

Seth nodded slightly, understanding Lance's frustration. "Aa suppose we're here t' defend our land, our homes and families. That's why A'm here," he concluded bluntly.

****

On the north edge of the camp, two dripping, hooded soldiers from a Cheshire regiment plodded across to Thomas Venables's tent and demanded to speak to him – their officer-in-charge. Grumblings in the ranks had reached a critical level, with desertion in mind. Venables permitted his two sergeants to enter and they hurriedly informed him of how a great many of their men were planning to sneak off in the night. Venables listened gravely. His natural good humour was already exhausted by many of his men's increasing reluctance and surly attitude to duty. He grabbed his cloak and sword and marched with his sergeants through the rain to where his unit was huddled. Summoning their attention, he angrily bellowed out his warning that any man deserting or quitting the field would, reaching home, have his abode burned to the ground and that he himself be hanged before his family. "I expect courage and loyalty from you all," he thundered, his face bulging red. "Do not disgrace yourselves with thoughts of cowardice!" He turned and stormed away, cloak flapping.

His audience stared after him. Usually seen as a genial man, his rant left them dumbstruck, in awe of his vile threat.

Breaking their silence, a single voice among the group was heard to moan. "He should try sleepin' out like us in the wet. He wouldn't be s' keen then on what's right and wrong."

There were mutterings of agreement as they hunched down again, bundled up against a further belt of stormy rain.

28

In an ante-room at Barmoor Tower, Surrey and the Lord Admiral sat discussing their strategy, going over details thoroughly in preparation for the council meeting with their leaders, summoned earlier to the residence. The assembly would be the last of its kind. Any others, the next day, could only be spontaneous, triggered by emergency. With their map and notes ready on the oak desk before them, they rose. Surrey regarded his son in silence before speaking in a sombre tone. "This time tomorrow it shall be done. Our fate will be decided. Our lives, yours and mine, depend upon victory." His face fell rigid, furrowing his aged, wrinkled skin. "We must not be taken captive. We succeed or we die. Do you understand?"

The admiral stared at his father, his lips pressed firmly together, and then he nodded. "I understand and I fear it not," he said quietly. In both men's eyes lay the unflickering beam of honesty and courage that their family blood demanded. At once, they hugged each other briefly; no other words were required.

Presently, the earl requested that they kneel side by side in prayer, which they did as one, lowering themselves at the desk's edge. They remained silent; their utterings private until they signed themselves with the cross, raised their heads and, ceremoniously, recited the Lord's Prayer together. Getting up from their knees, the old general strained to rise and his son moved quickly to assist him. "Let me be," insisted Surrey. Independently, he clutched the desk and, with a heave, hauled himself onto his feet. Still holding on, he flexed the stiffness in his knee joints before gathering his papers to go.

In the adjacent dining room, Surrey's war council had already gathered. Constable, Bulmer, Stanley, Dacre, Edmund Howard and their subordinate officers crowded round a large dining table, most of them standing. A strict solemnity showed in their faces. Straight-backed, they waited motionless for Surrey to enter the room accompanied by his elder son, the admiral, and leader of the English vanguard.

Heron's absence was deliberate. His advice had been given and he was inclined to avoid the disapproving glances of his detractors. Having sought permission from Dacre, he had removed some eight hundred cavalry riders from the squalid, crowded campsite to find shelter in the nearby ruined dwellings of Bowsden and Lowick villages. On the understanding that Heron had arranged for extra rations to be delivered to them from sources known to him, Dacre had agreed to it and insisted only that they return early, well before dawn.

Having spent more than an hour together preparing orders for the meeting, Surrey and his son entered the room with jaws clenched, and in frowned concentration, their appearance bearing the weight of their authority. A silent audience watched as the pair carefully laid out written papers and diagrams upon the table before them.

Resolute, the Earl of Surrey spoke first, thanking them for their patience. He then delivered his opening address, declaring the importance of their decision-making and how united they must be in their common aim of defeating the Scottish army. Stressing their commitment to fight the Scots, he summarised the intent with a brief and frank statement, which he read aloud.

"Gentlemen, one way or another, tomorrow we shall engage King James's army in battle. For King Henry, Queen Catherine and England, it is our purpose and duty to do so."

The message, short and unequivocal, was effective. Its finality shot true as an arrow across the room, striking the minds and souls of all gathered there. While the elderly earl slowly lowered himself into his chair, his son, the admiral, rose vigorously from his seat. The briskness of his movement mirrored the resolve that his father had declared.

"Before evening fell and the rain clouds descended, I observed for myself, across the river's valley, the enemy's camp on Flodden Hill. Our march this day has told them little. They remain on the height, uncertain of our intentions, dangling like puppets, waiting for the direction of our next move. Their position is established and strong; they will not relinquish it until they are sure we have gone from them or they believe we are on the march to block their retreat into Scotland. Crucially, the longer they stay on Flodden Hill, the more time there is for us to prepare our attack." He paused to check his notes upon the table.

"Any assault from this side is impossible. Nay, not impossible… utterly foolish; as useless as it would have been in the valley at Milfield, which has already met with our refusal. As we agreed earlier, our only reasonable chance of victory lies in an advance from the rear, on the raised land between Branxton and Flodden Hill. Up there, our position would not be disadvantaged and tactically, standing in their pathway back to Scotland, it would incite anxiety and perhaps fear in the hearts of many of their soldiers, desperate to return home."

He glanced round the company, underlining significance to what he was about to say. "It is not without peril, but we are strong and courageous and, God willing, shall overcome King James and his invading army." Engrained in his face and body, the admiral's obduracy transfixed his audience. There wasn't so much as a blink of an eye in the room.

When Lord Thomas had seated himself, his father slowly rose to his feet again. Surrey grimaced at the effort. His glare was haunting. "Tomorrow, before dawn, we must awake and, carrying only weapons, set forth on our route to cross the River Till once more."

To illustrate the journey he turned to a sketched map tacked onto the wall behind him. "The vanguard will set away first with the artillery from Bowsden, here, near us, and move west towards Duddo, then veer northwards to cross the bridge at Twizel."

He traced the way by means of a short stick held in his hand. "The rearguard will follow and make off towards crossing points upstream at Heaton Mill, here, and at Sandyford near Crookham village. On the rolling moorland west of the river we shall direct our march south to meet up at Branxton village, here, and in formation proceed to climb the hill on the south side of the village where we shall prepare our divisions for battle. Presently, your senior commanders – the Lord Admiral, Edmund Howard, Lord Thomas Dacre, Sir Edward Stanley, Sir Marmaduke Constable, Sir William Bulmer and myself – shall outline details of our troops' separate journeys and, particularly, how we shall traverse the marsh at Pallinsburn, which impedes our advance towards Branxton."

Surrey paused for a few moments to regain his breath and then turned fully to confront his audience. His voice seemed to crackle with emotion. "In truth, we are weary, all of us, and the morrow's challenge shall be daunting and severe. Yet we must rise above that. It is our honour to defend our country from a Scottish enemy allied to France – indeed, fighting for France. If we lead our men with a will that is bold and proud, we shall overcome the odds and achieve a just victory. Our soldiers are skilled and hardy. Inspire them to be fierce, to hold their ground and to fight with the power of gladiators." Surrey's craggy face flared avidly. "It is your task, each of you, come the new day, to rally your men to greatness; for them to become heroes in the history of our nation."

His entreaty met with a spontaneous stamping of feet, an acknowledgment of his rousing, eloquent speech. He raised his open hand in salute and, following a brief, united prayer led by Bishop Stanley, Surrey advised each division to gather separately in different rooms to finalise their aims so that, at dawn, they could mobilise their troops quickly and efficiently on the road to war.

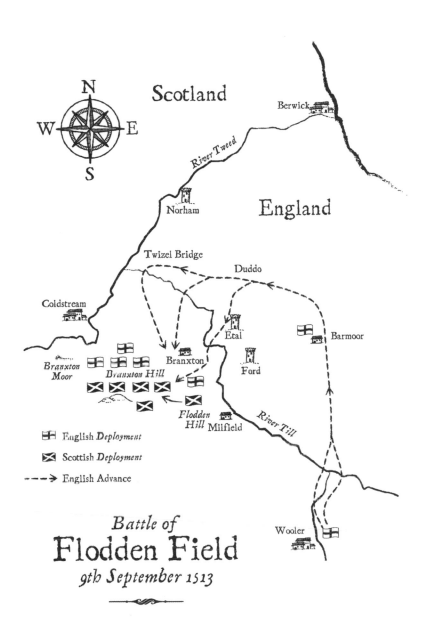

Battle of
Flodden Field
9th September 1513

29

It was a dark, sultry night. Low clouds blackened the earth. Rain fell continuously, turning from a fine drizzle to a shower then lightening again, though never ceasing. Across the English campsite, the huge area of sodden ground heaved and sighed with the noises of abject soldiers coughing, snoring, puffing and groaning in discomfort and misery. As if in a swamp that seethed with anguished and writhing creatures, nightmarish mutterings spluttered and rasped while, occasionally, stricken individuals roared and wailed, rending the air with sleepless outbursts.

At the first splinters of Friday's dawn, around four o'clock, shadows moved; figures, not yet identifiable, hustling about the heaps of men, waking and nagging and goading them from the ground to begin the long day. Curses and oaths of protest were voiced against the urgent calls to rise and prepare; orders were snapped and snarled to incite the listless, sleepy bodies into action. Small chunks of bread were handed out and spring water drunk reluctantly with distaste. Officers, captains and sergeants strode through the slouching crowds, bawling instructions and directions, assembling units into their divisions. Now, there was absolutely no doubt in the minds of lowly soldiers that, this very day, they were bound for battle.

Bills, lances, bows, arrow-filled quivers, swords, knives, axes and shields were collected or distributed from carts and wagons, and the artillery's guns and ammunition were hitched and latched onto horses, girthed and strapped to go. Whatever it was vital to keep dry remained wrapped. In the early hour's weary turmoil the anxiety-ridden soldiers were told to leave their belongings behind and each man to carry only the weapons and armour he needed for the fight. As the contours of the surrounding wilderness began to form in the murky light of pre-dawn, the grey, gnarled, stubble-faced hordes, braced with apprehension, shuffled like penitents into position, ready for the signal to begin their final march to Flodden.

The admiral's main vanguard was first to set off, followed by its two wings, trailing downslope towards the village of Bowsden, ransacked and deserted, where they proceeded to veer westwards away from the Berwick road. Close upon them there followed the rearguard under Surrey. Cushioned in his open carriage, he stared ahead with a stern, unyielding expression.

The dismal exodus lasted no more than an hour.

Save for Dacre's cavalry of just under two thousand Borderers, and those knights and men-at-arms too heavily armoured to walk any distance, the bulk of the twenty-two-thousand-strong army trod on foot, heads lowered in the dusky light, moving steadily along the seeping track rising across the bleak, bracken upland of Lickar Moor which lay to the north side of Watchlaw Hill and Etal Moor.

For morale's sake as well as guidance, Heron's local reiver men were chosen to accompany the leading group of each division. Throughout the ranks, their fierce reputation added an iron edge to the English army's audacious will. John Heron, distinct in black jacket, trousers, boots and red cape, rode at the very front alongside the Lord Admiral, directing the way. Even on a fine, sunny morning with clear visibility, the hilly country to the left of their lines would have concealed their course from Flodden's view. Still, the plan allowed that there would be no Scottish spies out this early, enabling the English army to push on, undetected.

For the first two miles the admiral and Heron were silent. A reserved respect existed between them; a mute understanding of each other – a sensibility strung to fact, rumour and instinct. Each endured private concerns other than those of the campaign: Thomas Howard's gravity in a failing, unhappy marriage, and Heron's bitter obsession with his critics and accusers, and their denunciation of his crimes and flight from justice. But what they had in common, which linked them more than anything else, was the urgent, lonely struggle inside them, to assert themselves, to prove to their societies that they were more than adequate, capable of living up to the expectation of family name and honour.

"Lord Dacre informed me of the death of Hinson, your main man. I offer my condolence," opened the Lord Admiral.

"He will be avenged," replied Heron chillingly, venom in his eyes.

"Of that I'm certain. There are many scores to settle this day. I pray God fires our passion and sustains us with good fortune." He turned to observe his companion squarely as they travelled. "What of your faith, John Heron?" he asked bluntly. "Do you believe that God will grant us victory?"

"Not if He favours the Scottish army more than ours," Heron answered sardonically.

The admiral sniffed in light dismay. "And why should He do that?"

Heron deflected the question with partial humour. "I, of all men, have least right to judge His reasoning, my Lord Admiral."

A devout Catholic, Thomas Howard studied him sympathetically. He believed absolutely that the power of God in a man like Heron would be a saving grace. "Promise, after the battle is won, to kneel alongside me in giving Him thanks," he proposed.

Heron realised quickly this was a request; a personal invitation he was unable to decline. It was in essence an appeal for solidarity between them – a hand of friendship.

"If it pleases you," he affirmed tonelessly.

Howard accepted it with a slight nod and brightness of eye. For a few moments he was intrigued as to how a man as fickle and devious, as Heron surely was, could also prove utterly dependable, even sincere, when carrying out his word. Or was this reliability merely temporary, convenient and useful until this conflict was resolved? No doubt, thought the admiral, this coming day and the next would provide an answer. Spurring his horse, he rid himself of his musing and they continued again in silence along the muddy track, the noise of wind and rain about them, and behind, the slosh-slosh-slosh of marching soldiers.

30

In the miserable early hours there was little chattering down the lines. Mindless from lack of sleep and energy, many of the soldiers were too tired to think and talk, marching dumbly to command like the teams of horses pulling the guns. However, as time wore on, their exertions generated a heat within them and their pulses quickened with the blowing of breath. With each passing mile a sense of rhythm absorbed their limbs and stirred their willingness to travel forward, like a stream perked by an increasing flow as its journey lengthened.

To toughen the infantrymen's desire for war, professional soldiers amongst the ranks shouted encouragement, bolstering their comrades' determination to persevere, to feel confident, and to believe without question in a fight that was theirs to win. Slowly, perceptibly, nervous faces that had been pale with exhaustion and gloom began to colour and tighten with purpose and intent, compacted into fierce, pointed stares of aggression.

Skirting around the destroyed tower at Duddo and the small, burnt-out hamlet that the Scots had ravaged in their wake when they'd secured the English countryside south of the River Tweed, the march continued across rough, bumpy, broom-patched moorland, avoiding the soft, marshy hollows.

Ahead, to their right, there came into view a circle of seven standing stones, planted on a small hill. Like sombre, petrified figures, they glared through the misty drizzle towards the front column of soldiers, which naturally slowed in curiosity and with some trepidation. It was quickly evident that this strange, unearthly aspect was breeding murmurs of nervousness; an echo of superstition that the men found instinctively disturbing.

Thomas Howard was immediately aware of the stones' portent, and how it might deter his army. "Tell me about them, quickly," he urged Heron.

Bastard Heron shifted in his saddle. "No one knows the truth of it, though it is said that tribes long ago placed them there. Maybe a site for burial or worship, as churches are today... or perhaps for sacrifice?"

"But what do local people say of them?" Howard asked in a cutting tone. "What do these stones mean to them?"

"Simple folk stay away from them, believing it to be a place of ill fortune," replied Heron. He shrugged his shoulders in a dismissive gesture. "Others see them with interest... a place of ritual and sorcery, like a witches' haunt, and so they visit them in darkness to contact the dead and other unworldly spirits."

It was exactly as the Lord Admiral feared. His jaw twitched in frustration. Nevertheless, it was too late to veer away and prevent his army's view of the stones. Balefully, he dreaded that the sight of them might tremble and shrink many a soldier's heart, already laden with apprehension. He shouted for his aides. "Move quickly, dress the stones in English colours – anything that will gird our men's faith in them!" he beseeched.

With some urgency, the riders rushed to the wagons and were soon galloping up the slope to the stone circle, where they hurriedly robed the stones in English flags and balanced helmets on top of each, transforming the monoliths into a parody of English sentinels.

The ruse proved effective – a distraction that amused and invigorated his soldiers. Chuckles and cackles trickled through the columns as they moved past the hill, and many raised their swords or bills in mock salute and called out in glee.

"The men are enlivened by it," observed Heron, intoning his approval of Howard's ingenuity.

The Lord Admiral stared ahead, unimpressed by Heron's compliment. "You failed to tell me about this place when we planned the route," he snapped, admonishing him.

"I laid no importance upon them, my lord," said Heron. "I see them only as stones but, now, I acknowledge that I was mistaken."

Howard glanced sideways at him. His expression softened. "I am pleased by your admission, John Heron, but on this day, of all days, we cannot have mistakes," he stated. He gazed forthright in a manner like that of his father. "Now, I believe we are approaching the point where our forces must divide. Yes?"

Heron momentarily caught the other's profile: the sloping brow; the slightly hooked nose; the small, concave mouth, and rounded, strong jaw. In the grandeur and resilience of this noble leader Heron simply noted the ardent look of a Howard.

"Yes," Heron replied, pointing to where the land rose a little before dropping away to the river, a quarter of a mile away at most. "My men know this and are ready to guide each column on its journey, as you instructed. We have done well to come so quickly these past five miles, despite the mud and water."

The admiral cleared his throat. "May the rest of this day go as well," he affirmed, his words coiled with characteristic self-assurance.

31

On Flodden Hill, King James woke abruptly, agitated by a strange, unsettling dream of Surrey, alone, riding through the Scottish camp on a giant hare, bawling obscenities at the massed ranks. Circling round the king's pavilion, the old earl had laughed uncontrollably before lolloping off downhill, unharmed by missiles hurled at him. Descending into the misty vale, he had crossed the River Till without a splash and vanished into the fog.

Exhausted, James climbed from his bed and dowsed his face in a basin of cold water. It was too early to rise. Lying down again, he dozed in and out of sleep for the next hour until impending dawn light and a squall of rain, slapping against his shelter, pulled his eyes open. He lay a while, pondering the strange and sinister image of his absurd dream. Since hares were, in folklore, believed to be an embodiment of evil, he felt unable to reconcile himself against the devilment it posed. From his bedside he reached for his cross of gold, which he wore daily, and kissed the pendant with devotion.

Out of bed, he kneeled and recited a short prayer before calling for his servant to help him dress. With the cross fastened around his neck and the chain belt tied about his waist – penance for his father's death, he dressed fully to confront the ultimate day.

Yet, unable to rid himself entirely of the unease invoked by the dream, King James was impelled again to kneel and briefly plead for God's courage, before he felt confident to venture outside into the dimness of a blowy, wet, grey early morning.

Across the hillside there was a slow stirring as the Scottish army shook itself, almost reluctantly, from another depressing night, cold and damp. Smoke from the campfires filtered and merged into the ashen dawn light that hung low in the sky like a stiff canvas awning. King James yawned and returned inside to be joined by his son, Alexander Stewart, the Archbishop, and seated side by side, they were served a modest ration of wheat bread with honey, and silver goblets of warmed wine.

"This is the day, my father, we have awaited. We have done all that is possible and I consider our duty done," said the Archbishop haughtily. Tall and regal, like his father, he exhibited his family's imperiousness.

His father gave him a weary look. "Once the hour of noon has been reached – the arranged time of battle – we shall decide upon our action. Until then we shall hold ourselves in readiness. On no account must discipline be relaxed."

"I agree, but there is in the camp a lighter mood among the troops, believing that Surrey has retreated and is on his way to the haven of Berwick."

James wiped his mouth with a cloth napkin. "I am unconvinced of it." His face looked strained. "Is there any news?"

His son seemed surprised by the request and cast a dubious look. "Not yet, my noble father, but of course, as soon as morning visibility allows it, a scouting party will set out at once. I suspect the English will not commence their march before mid-morning."

King James absorbed the logic of his son's claim; that it was too early for any news. Still on edge from his crazed dream, he was too embarrassed to describe it, even to his son. "Of course," he rejoined. "I realise I must remain clear-headed over such matters. Even so, I am the king and naturally over-mindful for the good of my men." Despite his effort, he was aware that his voice creaked with fatigue.

"I understand perfectly," the Archbishop answered precisely, bowing his head in reverence, though all too measured for it to be natural. Spoiled and favoured throughout his life, true emotions were inhibited by his bloated ego and future ambitions.

32

Beyond the standing stones, where the land starts to tilt towards the river, the English army came to a halt and messengers raced up and down the line with last-minute instructions. To enable the army to cross the River Till and not lose too much time, the advance became three-pronged. The bulk of the vanguard troops, including the artillery carriages, wheeled away first to the right, downriver, following the admiral and Heron, while Surrey's main rearguard drew forward, ready to continue straight on towards Heaton Mill. Far back, at the rear, Stanley's men and Dacre's, wings of the rearguard, were due to veer left before reaching Duddo, aiming for the two fords upstream, below the village of Crookham.

For the Earl of Surrey, this separation was a crucial stage of the journey; in reality, almost a point of no return. Despite his many years of combat experience, he groped at the significance of it with feelings of great responsibility and concern. Chief architect of this military manoeuvre, he knew the stakes were arguably higher than for any other challenge he had undertaken in the past. For his enterprise to fail was almost unthinkable; everything he had achieved in life would be jeopardised, including the safety of his sons, who would both surely die with him. No, he told himself, only victory is conceivable – only victory. And what's more, critically, in the kernel of his heart, he was convinced that it was truly possible, so steadfast was his faith in himself, his generalship, and in the power of his united army.

Driven by four black horses, Surrey's carriage bumped along the rough, uneven ground. Before leaving Barmoor, he'd insisted that the cover be removed for him to sit in the open, exposed to the elements and seen by his soldiers, fixed and resolved to an English victory; a triumph he'd sensed like a promise, from the very onset of their march from the Haugh at Wooler.

* * * *

Forging ahead, the vanguard made speedy progress northwards across fairly level, bushy, fertile ground towards the ruined Twizel Tower and the magnificent stone bridge below it, spanning the river. Built at the beginning of the century, the narrow, single-arched bridge allowed the guns and some twelve thousand troops to cross over the Till with slow, but secure progress during the mid-morning.

Meanwhile, a mile upstream, hardly an hour's march from Duddo, Surrey's train of soldiers cautiously descended the steep, slippery hill down to the river, which was gushing powerfully from the night's rain. On the other side of the river's hollowed bend stood the ravaged Heaton Mill, plundered and ruined by the Scots, its rough roadway ascending out of the ravine to the spoiled fortress of Old Heaton. With a chain of Heron's horsemen supporting the line, a section at a time, the soldiers waded cautiously through the current to the far side. The river here at the Millford was wider and deeper than the ford near Doddington and therefore more difficult to traverse. Aware of the risk, the columns of men stepped patiently and slowly through the splashing water, concentrating on making progress without mishap.

However, once across the swirling brown river, the men then had to struggle on wet, slippery feet up the steep, muddy road onto higher ground. The strain of this arduous and tedious challenge called for soldiers to rest at the top of the slope, which allowed the rear line behind, and its stragglers, to catch up and reassemble again before they could continue their march together.

The third and last approach to the river, by Dacre's cavalry of Border lancers (save for Heron's men) and followed by Stanley's slower foot soldiers, proved a lengthy business as they made towards Etal and the flat, marshy ground beyond which the river curved towards Crookham. The abnormal amount of late-summer's rain turned low, damp ground into a mire that was tricky and toilsome to march over. Consequently, their forced detours caused delays that had not been anticipated. The plaster of mud over foot and ankle simply added weight to legs already burdened by effort.

Nevertheless, by the latter part of Friday morning, the majority of the English army had managed to cross over the Till and was trekking onto the higher ground of Heaton Moor. On its open moorland, the troops swung southwards into the wind and drizzle, aiming towards the Pallinsburn and Branxton village, above which lay their destination – the hilltop.

33

Five abreast, the Elsdon men clumped together up the slope from the bridge at Twizel, sharing the crusts of greased bread they'd saved. Little Lance Milburn took one gulp then passed their last skin of beer to his nephew, Seth, who took a swig before handing it on to his brothers, Black Jack, Dick, and Samuel of Hepple Linn. Mossy Charlton and his brother Davie followed closely in the line behind along with three Hetheringtons, lanky-legged brothers from Harbottle. Grouped together, they were able to converse at will, encouraging one another, their confidence easily sustained.

Latterly assigned to old Sir Marmaduke Constable's division of mainly Yorkshiremen, they marched as a unit with other men from Northumberland under the Percy flag, with the haughty William and the elaborately armoured Lionel up ahead, astride their horses. Grouped according to the region in which they lived, it was practical, good soldiering for men from a locality to stick with those they knew, who spoke with an accent and dialect they easily understood. So Yorkshiremen from Ripon were surrounded by others from North Riding; Northumbrians from Redesdale ganged up with men from those parts, and so forth. It promoted fellowship and union, two factors that were inherent in maintaining morale and communication.

"A'm pleased w' didn't have t' plodge through the river and get w' feet soaked again," chirped Lance.

"Mine's a' right," replied Seth. "Aa layer mine wi' goose fat an' it keeps the water out," he explained.

"Me as well," answered Lance, "but when w' crossed the river at Doddington it came o'er the top o' the boot."

"That's because your legs are little," remarked Davie Charlton, attempting to joke.

The others smiled weakly, in no mood to laugh, and the funny side of it drifted away to nothing in the damp air. Tensions were growing, grating nerves. The spectre of battle was preoccupying their minds more and more, so that the basis of their speaking became mere opinion that did not require an answer. It was basic, banal talk, passing for conversation.

"We must've come nine t' ten miles a'ready," mused Dick Milburn who looked more like Seth than the other two brothers, but in a smaller frame.

"Aye, an' we've more yet t' go," said Seth.

"Another four at least," added Lance, "accordin' t' what A've heard."

"Maybe more," rejoined Mossy.

"Maybe," said Lance.

No one else joined in and the subject was dropped. They fell silent, staring above the helmets of those in front, their thoughts dipping apprehensively into the image of conflict awaiting them. Any sense of dread was screened behind stolid, flat expressions as they trooped up the worn slope, emerging from an avenue of elm trees onto open moorland beyond Tillmouth. Now, as their column turned into the wind, they could again feel rain spots prickling their faces. Heads down, they marched dourly onwards, the tramp of their footsteps setting the pace like a drum's laboured beat.

34

It was beyond mid-morning when a Scottish scouting party discovered the whereabouts of Surrey's army. Earlier, they had found the camp near Barmoor abandoned and had checked the road northwards to Berwick, but saw no sign of them. The clouded light of ceaseless rain, like mist, obscured their viewing from afar and only a careful search revealed the route that the English had taken, and their movement over the River Till.

On Flodden Hill, King James was livid when he learned of Surrey's advance westwards from Barmoor across the river, and he reproached himself for failing to heed his intuition and thus order his spies out much earlier. To ascertain for himself the approach of the English army, he called for his horse and swiftly led a party of his household guards northwards across the saddle of land between Flodden and Branxton Hill, roughly a mile away.

There on the hill's long, tilting ridge, facing Scotland, he caught a murky glimpse of two columns of English troops snaking their way over rolling land towards his position. Now almost noontime, he paused, his mind grappling with the emerging situation, his heart thudding in expectation of the inevitable encounter. The scheming, wily old earl, like a fox, had outsmarted him. The pain of indignation roared across his chest. With a torched look he turned his horse round towards Flodden and spurred off back to his army, accompanied by his staff, all braced by the grim reality of certain battle. Alarmingly, the English approach now barred any possibility of a direct retreat by the Scots towards the Tweed, and the notion preyed upon their thoughts like the hover of a hawk.

In their king's absence the Scottish commanders had frantically gathered inside the royal pavilion for his return. The pressing news of the English manoeuvre had prompted a haze of bafflement throughout the hill camp. No one knew for certain what the king's response would be to the threat. Until now, an attack from the rear had not been seriously contemplated and contingency plans had not been made.

Alarmed, his nobles waited for their monarch's return and his counsel. In his absence, they anxiously debated the dire circumstance thrust upon them and the options for engagement. Openly, Patrick Lindsay, Lord of the Byres, expressed again his latent fear of King James's positioning himself on the front line rather than a by-standing role as marshal of the field. The lords agreed in principle but were ever nervous of their king's resentment to this advice, which he had already vehemently opposed, recalling how he had vilified and banished the Earl of Angus.

A little later, when King James returned and took his seat amongst them, Lindsay boldly took it on himself to speak of their concern, softening the subject with fawning deference to his ruler.

"Good King, we your nobles strongly applaud your preparation of our army and its divisions. We acknowledge the skills of your leadership with great faith and are united in the cause. We are confident in achieving victory. We have a superior force and unrivalled cannon fire. But the greatest and most powerful weapon we have is a leader for whom we are ready to fight and even die for."

In order to maintain his poise, he inhaled deeply through his nose and continued earnestly. "To lose our king in battle would be to strip us of our swords and shields. It is therefore our dearest hope, Sire, that you reconsider your decision to lead your troops into action and freely position yourself at a place where you may deploy and govern our actions against the enemy. An enemy, dictated by a decrepit old earl, unfit even to serve food at Your Majesty's table."

An impending silence rounded the room, like the hushed anticipation of an axed tree, tottering on the verge of crashing to the ground.

James glared, eyes bulging. "My intentions have already been declared," he bellowed. "How dare you, Lord Lindsay, argue against me. If it were not for the moment, I should have you hanged. I shall fight as I choose – a man, a leader, and a king! If I stand alone for Scotland then I will not die a coward. Rile me no further, Lindsay, or your tongue will be slit in half!"

Overwhelmed by King James's rage, Lindsay bowed obediently. The other nobles observed their king's face, contorted with anger, slowly unfolding into a long, ponderous stare before he addressed them. His tone was imperial. "My lords, I have seen with my own eyes part of the English army heading towards us from the north. Our preparations here on Flodden Hill were focused on an attack from the south. We can choose to remain here and turn and prepare to face them, else, counter their approach by moving to meet them before they ascend the hill this side of Branxton village." He fell silent and, twisting the ring on his finger, he gazed around at them, his way of inviting comment.

"How much time have we, my king?" asked Lord Home, his nasal voice crackling with caution. Still bitten by his troops' humiliation at the strike of Bulmer's hidden bowmen near Milfield in August, he dreaded the thought of another upset.

"Two, possibly three hours, no more."

"Pray tell me, Majesty, what is to be gained by transporting ourselves to the other hill?" enquired his trusty Bothwell.

"If we allow the English to climb it and gather there, the advantage of high ground we have established here will be lost. I say we move at once, in all haste, onto Branxton Edge before they claim it," James insisted.

"Have we time?" asked Crawford.

"More time than Surrey's men," smirked the king, his confident manner assuring them, as it could. "The marsh and the hill's ascent will slow them considerably. But we must act swiftly!"

Since there were no further options, he promptly gave the initial order to Bothwell. "Instruct Borthwick to turn his guns at once and ensure he has whatever help he may require to drag them away. The rest of you, my true nobles, go forth immediately to your troops and mobilise them to march in haste, once my signal has been given. May God be with us."

His decisiveness gripped them. No one could argue. They crossed themselves in blessing then quickly departed the royal pavilion, leaving King James to pause alone, before he summoned inside the leaders and subordinates of his own central division and issued orders to abandon their hill fortress.

In the brief interlude, kneeling alone, King James clasped his hands together, closed his eyes and prayed to God for the strength to prevail, to show courage in leadership and, above all, claim victory for the pride and honour of his beloved Scotland. When he opened his eyes and the light of day flooded his vision, he felt the stirring of God's given power within him and stood up with a flourish. Steadying himself, he called and indicated to his servant that his officers, already lined up outside his door, should now enter.

35

When King James spied them earlier from Branxton Edge, the two leading columns of English soldiers were making a slow traverse of Heaton Moor. Though unable to ascertain which regiments they were, he presumed it would be members of Admiral Howard's vanguard, as his spies had forecast.

Were it merely a gathering of men travelling as a bunch into wind and rain, downcast, dishevelled and famished, it would have made a bleak, pathetic sight. But in their rugged thousands, purpose in their stride, obdurate and defiant, they displayed a formidable, pitiless aspect that was altogether different. Banners and horsemen at the fore, their lines appeared hostile and intimidating, like long-bodied serpents winding towards the narrow Pallinsburn valley.

Of course, at the time, James was incapable of knowing of the rearguard's delayed advance, but he knew of the Pallinsburn and that its boggy ground posed a severe obstacle to the English approach, a delay that would allow him sufficient time, should he decide to move his own army to confront them.

****

At the head of their separate columns, both Edmund and Thomas Howard had been given ample warning of the elongated marsh that stretched across their path towards Branxton village. Heron had also advised how the recent wet, stormy weather would have extended it. Other than a narrow, stony causeway across its middle, known locally as the 'Branx Brig' – the Branxton bridge – that the Lord Admiral's troops and his artillery intended to navigate, Edmund Howard's division was directed to circumvent the bog to the west, while Surrey's rearguard formations were due to skirt round the eastern end of it, beside Crookham. As with their crossing of the swollen Till, the venture across the mire was hazardous, hampering their progress and prolonging the disconnection of Surrey's army, which had split up shortly after passing the seven standing-stones at Duddo.

Although unaware of the king's personal observation of their progress, the admiral was certain by now that news of his approach would have reached the Scottish camp. He trusted that the confusion it brought would, initially, cause a quake of dilemma and a period of indecision that would enable the English formations sufficient time to reunite and then climb Branxton Hill, ready to engage the enemy. He also prayed that panic would branch throughout the Scottish camp, causing trepidation and doubt to dent their soldiers' confidence.

Somewhere he'd heard it said that an army daunted was an army half-conquered. It seemed an obvious, trite remark at the time, but not so now.

Logically, he appreciated that the encircling march was a bold move netted with risk, but it was only as the hill grew closer and more visible that Admiral Howard realised how exposed his troops would become, ascending the bare height. Suddenly, he felt the scratching of danger in his chest and, grave, he turned his gaze to his right, checking on the progress of his brother, Edmund, leading his train of men half a mile away to the west, lumbering dimly through a lash of rain. Although his younger brother infuriated him at times, he secretly admired his pluck and carefree nature. Yet he lacked military experience and the admiral worried for his survival in the fight ahead.

"I believe it is your big man, Straughen, that rides beside my brother. He looks comical seated upon a pony," the admiral jibed.

Heron looked past the admiral in his fine armour and could make out Straughen's large, outlined figure propped up in the saddle, like a dummy rider meant to magnify the size of the column. "Though his mount is sturdy enough, he's been cajoled many times to seat a bigger horse. But he's a stubborn man," despaired Heron, lightly, shaking his head.

"My brother was adamant to choose him as his guide. I suspect he thinks of him, superficially, as a friendly giant. He does appear so."

"Indeed he does, at times, but like a tame bull he can turn. When enraged he has the strength of Hercules," Heron replied, then raised both hands to adjust the strap of his steel helmet. He went on, "I've seen him lift a fully grown man above his head as though he were a sack of cloth, and hurl him to the ground."

Thomas Howard noticed again the protective metal strips affixed to Heron's leather gauntlets, but made no comment. He was curious to know of their creation but considered it imprudent to pester him with another of his questions. Only yesterday he'd enquired why he wore a red cape and Heron had hesitated before mumbling a reply, saying it had been his mother's favourite colour. Leaving his interest aside, the admiral encased himself once more in the challenge ahead, and the imminent course of their bloody action.

36

Jock Burn chided his three sons, Dody, Wullie and Ewan, urging them to abandon their game of dice and hurry to prepare for war. Their eyes sparked with excitement as they harnessed themselves in jackets and helmets. Brimming with enthusiasm, they elbowed each other and grinned at the grim-faced seriousness of others in their section – Burns, Taits and Youngs, who mingled around them.

Combing back his long, lank hair with one hand before donning his helmet, Andrew Tait regarded their levity with suspicion. "Only young callants like you would be smirkin' at what's happenin'," he said, frowning. "Y'u might be soon wishin' you'd bust a leg like y' brother, Tucker, an' be headin' back hame with him now, away from a' this."

Earlier that Friday morning, before news of the English march had dashed over them, monks had decided that the injured Tucker should leave for home. They could do no more for him stranded on Flodden Hill. He required rest and attendance, best found at home with his mother and two sisters. His father, Jock, unsure of the day's events, had arranged for a cart and pony to carry his invalid son, steered by an elderly neighbourman who had helped to cook for them in camp. In saying his farewell, Jock, at the time ignorant of the English encircling march and anticipating that the Scottish army would be disbanded early afternoon, suggested that he might even catch up with them on the way back.

The three remaining brothers looked blankly at Andrew's gaunt expression, deaf to his warning, and answered his pessimism with a casual shrug of their shoulders. Naively, they were not nervous about fighting an English force that they had yet to see, and which they had heard scoffed at for seeming much weaker.

In a matter of minutes, when everyone in their unit appeared to have been rounded up, the Taits, Burns and Youngs set off together with other bands, quickly striding out to an area designated for regiments under Lord Home's leadership where they would be organised and briefed to march.

On the grassy southern slope of the hill, the hundreds of grazing oxen had been hurriedly herded together and driven up towards the gun emplacements, where scores of heaving men and horses had already turned the weapons. As soon as the teams of oxen were yoked and hitched, their drovers urgently beat them with sticks and the beasts, grunting with effort, ploughed forward through the mud, dragging the huge, trundling cannon slowly round the hill onto its northern slopes.

In just over an hour, the dull inertia of the wet hill had erupted into swirling, noisy rivers of men foaming and eddying into their respective battalions, covering a vast, open swathe of ground. Ranked in their thousands, the four separate divisions and their reserve, at the given signal, commenced their short journey of just over a mile, across the shallow basin of upland moor dipping between Flodden and Branxton Hills.

Unlike the English army, the Scots had the streaming rain and wind at their backs, so they could march with their heads raised, like the proud points of the pikes they held aloft as they dragged the butt ends over the ground behind, each spear roughly the length of three tall men lying in a line. In their coloured uniforms, plaids and armour, with flags and banners unfurled, the Scottish divisions created a colossal, awe-inspiring sight – an army well over thirty-thousand strong; clansmen, levies and servicemen, united behind their proud king, his nobles and chieftains from throughout Scotland.

Strangely, though their advance was properly marshalled, disciplined and orderly, there seemed a twisted irony in heading homewards to encounter the English force they had ventured south to meet. So close to the Border, it thrummed ominously in the consciousness of those whose passion to fight had deflated the night before, when the battle had seemed unlikely. Repeating themselves, like the patter of raindrops upon their helmets, the grave words tapped repeatedly inside their heads: this was not meant to be... this was not meant to be...

37

Unaware of the Scottish army's mobilisation, Lord Admiral Thomas Howard continued to lead his vanguard troops, descending into the lower vale of the Pallinsburn, which was smeared in rain. A trusted messenger named Simmons had informed Howard of his father's fording the river, but as yet there was no sight of his troops advancing on the left, presumably slowed by a difficult crossing.

On his right, his brother Edmund's columns had branched away to the west in order to round the bog. As they faded from view behind a low, arched hill, the admiral felt acutely the isolation of his situation. At this point, the separation of the English divisions from each other snapped heavily on his thoughts, like a yoke collar clamped over a beast's shoulders to drag a plough.

Wheeling his horse around, he halted his entourage to enable the lines behind to close up. He waited impatiently, fumbling with the reins; his stare was solid and implacable. The artillery carriages clanked closer, headed by Nicholas Appleyard, acting Master Gunner. Thomas Howard rode back, unaccompanied, to demand that they might go faster. "My lord," Appleyard remonstrated in dismay, "the horses are struggling already even with the foot men we have assisting, pushing and pulling alongside. I fear we can go no faster."

"Then use more men, but keep up!" Howard ordered, abrasively. His command was uncompromising. He wheeled his mount sharply and returned to the front of the column.

Trudging miserably into the rain, heads bowed, the front column rounded a wood and cut down through bracken towards an expanse of marsh lumped with ancient, twisted trees, reeds and ferns.

Alone, Heron rode ahead, picking his route along a soft but firm pathway towards a dense, dingy centre. The line behind thinned out, following his steps. The bog oozed with a smell of decay. His and the admiral's party came to a channel of foul, moving water – the burn – and the narrow stone bridge over it. Painstakingly, each of the twenty-three field guns had to be hauled across in turn, proceeding slowly onward along an earth-raised causeway, funnelling into the open. On the far side of the morass the order was given to turn right and keep moving along the edge of the narrow dene, under cover, to allow room for the entire division to assemble in the shallow valley, out of view of the village. There, the instruction was for them to remain and wait until the lengthy task of traversing the bog was accomplished by all sections.

Now that the day was slipping towards mid-afternoon, the admiral and his knights grew more agitated for news of the others. It was therefore much to their relief when a Border rider from Edmund's division appeared at full pelt from upstream to announce that they had rounded the bog and were channelled in the dip, awaiting orders.

"Stay where you are, out of sight. We shall soon march up towards you," commanded the Lord Admiral, with a look of exasperation. "Tell your leader, my brother, that this was the order he was given," he added impatiently. The rider, Foxy Tom, one of the brash Dunne twins, glanced at Heron – his chief, saluted him and rode off without any deference to Howard's authority. The admiral stared at Bastard Heron. "I conclude that your men are commonly rough-looking, stubborn, vulgar and uncouth fellows," he remarked with scorn.

Heron appeared untouched by the insult. "They are indeed, my lord. It's in their nature, I suppose," he answered glibly, as if it were a quality, not a fault.

"Good manners and decency can be to a man's advantage," mocked Thomas Howard. He sniffed, as he tended to do when either amused or slightly ruffled, then nudged his horse away to speak with an officer who was galloping towards them.

The young knight, whom the admiral recognised, was Robert Norton, a nephew of Sir Sampson Norton, Master of the King's Ordnance, fighting with His Majesty's army in France.

"My lord," Norton blurted, yanking his sorrel-coated stallion round.

Flustered, his words flew out of a dry mouth. "The last gun to cross the bridge slid off the pathway and overturned, injuring two of its crew. We've managed to haul the gun upright but one of the men who was trapped beneath is badly hurt."

"And the other?"

"Only bruised and sore, my lord, thank goodness."

"Is the gun still capable of firing?"

"The soft ground prevented any damage. Master Gunner assures me it will function properly once cleaned." Norton paused to catch his breath. "But the injured crewman will be lucky to survive. We've lost a valuable man," he concluded dismally.

Admiral Howard stared at the young knight's downcast expression. The incident seemed to embrace the dangers of their advance and the predicament they faced. "See that he is given any comfort you can offer." He paused, his eyes straining. "Now, young man," he said spikily, "Lift your spirits; go back and hasten your unit to join us. Do you understand?" he ended sharply.

Robert Norton blinked, self-consciously. He straightened himself in the saddle. "Yes, sir," he replied and then stoutly swung about and raced off.

38

Early afternoon, on the east side of the River Till, Dacre and Stanley were frustrated by the slow pace of their march. Last to depart from the overnight camp at Bowsden, their foot soldiers, at the end of the army's line, found themselves slipping and slogging over ground already mud-churned by the trod of the thousands ahead of them. This effort alone caused them to fall behind. After they had turned from the dividing routes taken by the Howards, near Duddo, their journey to Etal had been hampered by pools and marshes they had not entirely expected. On principle, or pride, Lord Dacre had bullishly refused to use any of Heron's local men as navigators, believing he knew the route well enough. He began to rue that decision when they were forced to make several detours around flooded hollows in the Till's flat valley floor, south of Etal.

After a number of Stanley's recruits, suffering already from sickness and hunger, collapsed from exhaustion, other worn out soldiers grabbed the opportunity to rest while these wretched men were revived. One of them, unable to regain consciousness, and slowly dying, was left behind with a cousin to see him out and then bury him. Beginning to panic that they might fail to join up with the rest of the army in time at Branxton, both lords agreed that Dacre and his cavalry should press on to Sandyford, leaving Stanley's slower infantrymen to follow as fast as they could manage.

****

Meanwhile, downstream, on the west side of the River Till above Heaton Mill, Surrey's main rearguard had fully gathered to recommence its march towards Crookham. The old earl had hoped to spot soldiers from his sons' battalions on Heaton Moor, but to no avail. He dreaded his own regiment's lateness and, adding to his consternation, Surrey sensed a reluctance seeding in the lethargy of those about him. Crabby-faced, he barked orders for his leaders and knights to gather round him, whereupon he again voiced his intent to fight against the Scots who had allied themselves with France. "This very day we shall meet the enemy in battle," he vouched, "and fight like Englishmen, for our king and country. I urge you, nay, I implore you, to do your duty and may it be supreme. Never forget, our country has been invaded. England has been invaded and we, together, shall defend it!" he echoed defiantly.

It was by no means an eloquent speech but his avowal, delivered with typical conviction, proved uplifting and his party answered vociferously: that they would fight for him as well as for their king. The nature of their tribute was confirmation again of the verve and power in the old earl's leadership, which he accepted typically with modest grace. Relaying his words to their respective units, the exhausted foot soldiers were fortified by them too and set off again, hearts pumping with renewed energy and grit, rejuvenated by their general's vision that each and every one of them should be their country's saviour.

39

On the easy slope behind the crest of Branxton Hill's long, tilted top, King James and his Scottish commanders deployed their separate regiments into 'plumps' or blocks of pikemen, known as schiltrons. Time-pressed, they moved apart according to design, stretching out into four main divisions.

Home's Border men and Huntly's Highlanders, roughly eight thousand, combined on the left. Centre-left consisted of a slightly higher number of pikemen under the three earls – Crawford, Errol and Montrose, while the largest division was led by the king himself and took centre-right, numbering over ten thousand. Flanked on their right, completing the front line, stood three thousand Gaelic clansmen from the Highlands under Lennox and Argyll, armed with their traditional weapons, claymores and axes, rather than long pikes. Lastly, Bothwell's reserve division, to the rear of centre, numbering about three-thousand-strong, included Count d'Aussi and some of his Frenchmen.

In these formations the great Scottish army awaited further orders, its action dependent upon news of the English advance from spies that King James had sent creeping over the ridge of the hill.

It was at this stage that these phalanxes of Scottish soldiers found themselves increasingly engulfed and irritated by heavy, grey-black smoke. After they had departed from Flodden, the camp followers, in much haste, had begun to set fire to the huts, tents and shelters, housed with bedding straw, that clustered the hill. Piling all the other accumulated rubbish such as blankets, animal hides and garments onto the flames, the damp, filthy items spawned billows of turgid smoke that sailed in the wind like galleys, pursuing the departed troops.

Although at first disconcerted by the huge pall of thick smoke enveloping the hillside, fouling the very air they breathed, the king's annoyance was rapidly overtaken when he learned of the English front labouring across the marsh. Now, suddenly, he felt fate on his side, providing him with a golden opportunity to move his army forward, screened by the lingering fog of smoke. Without delay, he gave orders for all on horseback to dismount, leading by example, and for the entire army in its formations to march on foot over the wide summit of the hill, onto its northern, forward slope.

****

Below, out of sight in the shelter of the narrow dene on the south side of the bog, the English vanguard was by now mostly hustled into line waiting with uncertainty for the arrival of Surrey's central rearguard, and his two wings led by Dacre and Stanley. Observing the dense layer of smoke covering the ridge of Branxton Hill, the admiral swiftly held a meeting with his supporting commanders, Sir Marmaduke Constable, Sir William Bulmer, and his brother, Edmund Howard.

"It appears the Scots are preparing to abandon camp on Flodden sometime this day, or even tomorrow morn," the admiral stated. "Or else, as Sir William has surmised, knowing of our encircling advance, as surely they must, the fire's smoke is being used as a means to thwart and perplex our army's ascent while they ready themselves for battle, turning about to face us. What say you both?"

"I say we ascend the hill at once, my Lord Admiral, as planned," said Edmund, urgently.

"I agree," old Sir Marmaduke concurred. "I believe it is imperative that we secure the hill as soon as we can, with or without the rearguard. The smog cannot last." His wise composure was gladly reckoned in the absence of their father, the Earl of Surrey.

Thomas Howard nodded. "Then we must act immediately. I shall order Heron to gather a troop of his fiercest men to join us at the fore. See to your captains that they mobilise their units," he urged.

"Why Heron, my Lord Admiral?" complained Bulmer, his eyes flaring with resentment.

The admiral stared at Sir William as if he should know better than to question his decision. "Because I say it," he chastened him.

Bulmer paused, pursed his lips, shrugged his shoulders in obeisance and said no more.

Within minutes, supported by his three trusty commanders, armoured nobles, men-at-arms and Heron's toughest fighters, the admiral led the first foray out of the hollow, riding up the grassy slope towards the abandoned village. They had barely ventured more than a hundred yards when, to their shock, the smoke's veil began to lift and they saw for the first time the whole of the Scottish host ranged across the skyline ahead of them, occupying the ground that they themselves desired to hold.

"God in Heaven!" exclaimed the admiral, reining in his horse. The contingent halted in amazed horror. To their alarm, there was a boom of cannon, the balls whistling above them and crashing beyond the Pallinsburn marsh. In terror and disarray, the entire outfit spun round and dashed back to the safety of the dene where most of the thousands of soldiers cowered on the ground, quaking in terror. Even when the explosions ceased, many remained lying, face down, too petrified to move, whilst others, scrambling onto their feet, yelled at comrades to follow as they raced off to hide behind trees that ringed the bog.

"Calm the men! Calm the men!" the Lord Admiral roared again and again, galloping along the dene, demanding his instruction be carried out by the captains and sergeants of the units. "We are safe here. Tell them!" he bellowed. "Keep order! Keep order!"

In desperation he shouted for Simmons, a superior horseman and one of the Howard family's most valued aides. The tiny, pale-faced and thin-shouldered rider came to him at once. "Here!" Howard implored, having snatched the chain holding his Lamb of God medallion from about his neck. "Go… find the earl at once and give him this. He'll understand. Ask that he joins us in all haste, for the Scots stand above us and, alone, we cannot match them!"

Clutching the charm, Simmons tore off downstream towards Crookham, leaning low in the saddle, fearful that the now silent Scottish guns might resume their firing.

40

On top of the hill, Robert Borthwick, the Scottish Master Gunner had pleaded that his heavy guns be permitted to continue firing towards the English tail, still visibly trailing across the bog. But James refused his request on grounds of chivalry and the need to preserve his stock of gunpowder for the battle proper.

Borthwick's exasperation was shared by several leaders who believed the bedraggled English were vulnerable in number and might. Errol and Bothwell even urged King James to attack at once down hill, convinced the English could be easily overwhelmed, but their king's valour was set upon a fight that was to be pitted fairly, equal to both sides. Having regained the initiative by moving his army across from Flodden to maintain the advantage of higher ground, James was in no hurry to forsake it with an impetuous attack on an enemy that had yet to show itself fully – and the hand it concealed.

"I shall have them all before me in plain view before I commit to our actions," he responded shrewdly, regally dismissing their argument. Magnificent in full armour, James stood upon the upper slope with his powerful, glorious army spread across a mile of hilltop, bristling like wolves, hungry for the slaughter of the timid flock sheltering below.

****

Remaining in the small valley, the English vanguard waited nervously, daunted by the awesome Scottish guns and the vast army poised on Branxton Hill. Despite their officers' show of confidence and the professional soldiers' unflinching stare, the levies felt doom, like a beast, breathing down upon them and the sweat of fear rolled down their chests.

Displaying his leadership, the admiral trotted his horse up and down the lines repeatedly, willing the rearguard's appearance. For the benefit of all he passed, his regard was both patient and cool. He was aware that his predicament teetered on the possibility of an immediate Scottish assault, but he trusted that King James's caution would prevail. Behind his calm countenance Thomas Howard's heart pleaded for God's mercy. And, as if in answer, his consternation was suddenly diverted by a loud voice. "Look, my lord!" shouted William Percy, riding quickly to his side. "Heron has ridden out, alone. Did you order it?"

Irate, the admiral swung about and galloped up out of the dene, with Percy and Edmund close behind, followed by their guards. Going no further than the rise, they could see Heron riding past Branxton village church towards the hill presided upon by the immense Scottish army. "He's either a traitor or a mad fool!" exclaimed Percy.

Thomas Howard spied Straughen, the big man, in their group and summoned him. "What in Hell's fire is Heron thinking?" he cursed aloud. "His duty is to remain with us and his troops."

Appearing unruffled by the fuss they were making, Straughen wiped his nose with the back of his hand. "Maybe he wants a fight wi' any Scot that dares t' face him, man t' man," he said bluntly.

"Heron is not our champion," Lord Howard blasted.

"He's ours though," replied Straughen with a biting edge to his tone. "An' every Border man knows it, on both sides."

"I do believe, Lord Thomas," interjected his younger brother, "that

Heron's aim is simply to occupy the enemy whilst we wait for the rearguard to join us." Edmund Howard turned sharply to reproach William Percy. "I also know for certain that he is neither a fool nor a traitor."

The sound of an approaching horseman turned their heads. It was Simmons, the thin-shouldered messenger who had been despatched earlier, clutching the admiral's medallion. Between breaths, Simmons reported anxiously that Lord Dacre and the Earl of Surrey were about to join the vanguard though Stanley's contingent was still to show, delayed by marshland. However, Simmons added, a forerunner from the Lancashire regiment had assured him that they were close to fording the river and promised they would arrive in due haste.

Grim, the Lord Admiral considered the news before turning to glare at Straughen. "Stay about the field, and when it is done bring Heron to me, alive or dead," he snapped, then, followed by the others, he set off back down to the dene, eager to be there to greet his father, and Lord Thomas Dacre.

Alone on horseback, watching them leave, Straughen scratched his groin and gave a yawn. Turning his horse about to face the hill, he put two fingers to his lips and whistled loudly enough for Heron to know that he was there.

41

Riding over a small ridge that inclined towards Piper's Hill, Heron heard the signal as he cantered his speckled roan down a short slope to the foot of Branxton Hill, where he followed the muddy burn upstream along the dip. On the crest of the hillside above him to his left loomed the entire Scottish army. Coming to a halt below the banners of Lord Home's Border regiments positioned on the western side, Bastard Heron stood up in the saddle and brandished his sword defiantly, daring anyone to fight. Distinctive in his red cape, he was certain that he would be instantly recognised and that his challenge would be met.

It wasn't long before a single figure strode down the slope to halt on the other side of the stream. It was Archie Tait, in leather jerkin and helmet. Demonstrating his contempt, he held Hinson's sword aloft, flaunting his prize. "Is this what you're after?" he mocked.

Heron dismounted, stepping closer, and glared. "What's your name?"

"A friend t' the Kers," the Scot boasted.

Heron observed the green glint of his eyes and was sure that he was a Tait. "Archie Tait," he muttered hatefully.

"Aye, it's me all right," Archie gleamed.

Heron perceived the daring confidence of a young, adventurous man desperate for self-acclaim; a Scottish reiver, ambitious for the fame he'd gain by slaying the Bastard of Ford – wanted and reviled throughout the Marches of Scotland's Border lands for the murder of Sir Robert Ker.

Heron gripped his sword and shield and stepped warily across the soggy ground and its narrow waterway. The two adversaries confronted each other, preparing to duel. Almost as a preliminary introduction to their fight, they glared briefly in silence, both men absolutely rigid.

Archie Tait was first to move. Weaving Hinson's sword between them, his blue-green eyes sparkled with excitement. Tentatively, they parried, circling while assessing each other's stance and style of combat. Though the younger man moved agilely behind his shield, with a spring in his legs, Heron's energy seemed contained, his face set with concentration. And despite his heart baying for vengeance, he curbed the instinct, staying hunched in readiness to defend himself.

Tait whipped a side slash, which Heron's sword blocked in time, and then a second blow curving downwards that Heron's shield deflected. The dashing young Scot attacked once more with a lunge that was clubbed away, again with shield. The pair squared up as before, feinting and jabbing blows. Tait was skilful and remarkably fast. Heron remained patient, yet to be the aggressor.

The young Scot grinned then launched another combination of strokes and strikes that Heron defended rigorously. Ducking under the last of these blows skimming his head, Bastard Heron backed away, as if in retreat from the other's ferocity.

"You tire easily," hissed Archie in mockery. His face beamed as his breath steamed faintly in the damp air.

Heron eyed him silently, his chest rising and falling as he filled his lungs with damp air. Even though Tait's swordsmanship appeared to dominate, delivering multiple strokes from all angles, which were strenuously deflected, Heron, with all his experience, had by now already perceived a frailty in his enemy's fight. After a direct thrust, Tait would let his blade drop fleetingly in withdrawal before swinging it upwards again for use. For a split second, Heron surmised, this habit exposed him to a sudden downward stroke.

For the first time, Heron made the initial move. As if to show Tate that he had energy left, it seemed, he flailed the air between them, though out of range. Archie grinned, dropping his arms, inviting further action. "You'll need to come closer, Heron, if y'u dare t' fight me like a true man," he scoffed, his handsome face radiating confidence.

Stepping forward, Heron cunningly raised his sword head-high, flicking the air, angling his own shield a fraction to expose his body. Tait saw the opening and lunged, fast as a lizard's tongue. In anticipation, Heron snapped shut the gap in time and before Tait's lowered sword came up to defend himself, Heron sliced his blade down into the hollow between his opponent's neck and shoulders. As Archie Tait's legs buckled and he staggered with a look of astonishment, Heron flashed his sword again across his opponent's thigh above his long boot, raking it open and the young Scott dropped to the ground, mouth agape, snorting in agony.

At once, Heron leapt in and swiftly stamped on Tait's arm, enabling him to wrench Hinson's sword free from his grasp. Deliberately, using it and not his own, he delivered the fatal stab into the body. There was a final rasp of air, then Archie Tait lay motionless on his back, staring skyward, mouth twisted, green eyes gaping blankly – the beautiful face no more.

Squinting up at Home's company, hovering on the hill's slant, John Heron retreated promptly to his horse. Mounted, he paused, reflecting upon the deed and the satisfaction of his revenge. Reining his stallion about he rode away, veering towards the raised mound of Piper's Hill that banked along towards the small village church.

It was there, in the drizzle, that Straughen had witnessed the duel and was now waiting for him. He grinned with approval at Heron's triumph but said nothing of the feat, as if it had been expected. "Surrey and Dacre have joined us at last," he announced. "But Aa have to say the admiral is far from happy with y'u. But mind, his brother spoke up against William Percy who faulted y'u for ridin' off y'self without permission."

Heron showed no reaction to any of this. Instead, he handed over Hinson's bloodstained sword. "Here, my friend, use it well," he exhorted.

Straughen received the sword with hesitation and an uncertain frown. He could not recall Heron ever having called him 'friend' before. For a moment the word floated like a spark in his mind. He held up the sword and thought of Hinson, and of the position that was now entrusted in him – Straughen – to uphold.

Heron spurred his horse away. "Come on," he shouted impatiently, and together they cantered back down towards the small valley on the north side of the bog where, out of view, the English army was massed.

Battle Positions

 English *Deployment*

Scottish *Deployment*

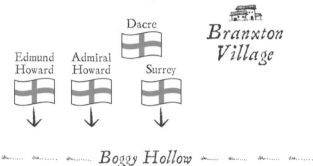

Dacre

Branxton
Village

Edmund
Howard

Admiral
Howard

Surrey

Boggy Hollow

Stanley

Home &
Huntly

Crawford
Errol
Montrose

King James

Lennox
& Argyll

*Branxton
Hill*

Bothwell

N

W   E

S

Battle of
Flodden Field
9th September 1513

42

The Lord Admiral and his father, the Earl of Surrey, were hurriedly counselling their commanders when Heron and Straughen returned. Consequently their arrival was ignored in the urgency of the meeting.

Reunited, the old general and his eldest son had swiftly decided to reorganise their forces in order to confront the Scottish army's four visible divisions. This required moving a number of troops from their original contingents to supplement other regiments. Pressed by a lack of time and the congestion of thousands of men milling in the small vale, it was a tricky and bold undertaking, one that tested their military judgement to the full.

To oppose Home and Huntly's battalions, Edmund Howard's right-wing division was swelled to well over three thousand soldiers from Northumberland, Lancashire and Cheshire. On their left, marines from the admiral's ships were joined by more units from Constable's levies from East Riding, William Percy's Northumbrians, and the Bishop of Durham's troops led by Sir William Bulmer. To galvanise their efforts, Saint Cuthbert's banner was to be carried proudly at the fore by Lord Lumley's men. This increase of men enlarged the admiral's division to roughly eight thousand against the Scottish earls – Crawford, Errol and Montrose. To the left of centre, to confront the king's largest division, Surrey's retainers and levies were joined by several of Constable's contingents from Yorkshire, bolstering his force to around seven thousand soldiers. Stanley's companies of some three thousand men, on arrival, were due to form up on the left wing to counter the smaller battalions of Highlanders on the Scottish right, commanded by Lennox and Argyll. Finally, Lord Dacre was ordered to hold in reserve his cavalry of nearly two thousand Border men, concealed behind the two central divisions; this included Heron's raiders.

Although outnumbered in every case, Surrey, sternly obdurate, believed his army – made up of levies that regularly practised weaponry skills, alongside many trained, experienced soldiers – to be capable of withstanding the Scottish might, much of which consisted of novice military men from the far-off regions of their country.

The mobilisation of the English regiments, under pressure, demonstrated the disciplined structure of the Howards' command. Out of the confusion and turmoil of a crowded corridor, the separate formations were reassembled and organised in a remarkably short time.

Since the afternoon was slipping away, Surrey concluded that the wait for Stanley could not continue. Without proclamation or pomp, he uttered his order to advance and with horns blasting, the English army began its climb out of the Pallinsburn valley. Ascending the sloping land away from the boggy hollow, they toiled up towards Branxton village, and then continued onto the rise that stretched along from Piper's Mount, where each division filed off towards its designated position.

Meanwhile, lining the crest of Branxton Hill, an estimated thirty-three thousand Scots glowered down through the rain, their intimidating aspect weakening the legs of those Englishmen whose hearts shuddered in dread of pain and death.

Astride their mounts on the back slope of Piper's Hill, Lord Dacre chanced to remind Heron of his earlier agreement to obey him and rebuked his independent act of vengeance. "You ought be aware that the Earl of Surrey is also much disappointed that revenge governed your senses, more so than your allegiance to higher authority."

Dacre's scowl slowly faded. He stared up at the enemy ranged along the skyline, like the teeth of a woodcutter's saw. "But it is done," he said, gruffly. "Perhaps in battle you may prove yourself more reliable."

"I shall endeavour to do so, my Lord Dacre," Heron replied calmly. "Even if death be my reward," he added, irony in his tone.

Lord Dacre, determined that he would have the final say, displayed his superiority by pointing an assertive finger at Heron, chafed by the man's seeming lack of remorse. "Let victory be our reward!" he chided. "See to it, Heron. See to it, man!"

43

King James had seen the one called Heron seeking revenge; it was an unfortunate event, beyond his immediate control – a matter of barbarian honour between Border villains. Whomsoever he'd killed, however, was of no consequence.

Vainglorious, King James stood surveying the English army spreading itself below into opposing divisions. He glowed in anticipation. Now, at last, he felt he had them at his disposal and his powerful cannon could begin a successful bombardment of the weaker English guns. After destroying them, his artillery could then turn its aim to blast and shred holes through the ranks, reducing them to chaos whereupon his Scottish divisions would sweep down upon them, like the wind and rain, wiping them from the field. He savoured this vision of the enemy's destruction with contained glee.

In a state of cold excitement, James removed the gauntlet from his left hand to reveal Lady Heron's opal brooch, pinned to his sleeve, and the French queen's turquoise ring worn around his little finger. Intuitively, he raised his arm and kissed the brooch as if it were a good luck charm. For a fleeting, overflowing moment, he imagined her face, her tender smile, her lips, her hands outstretched towards him, wanting him again to embrace her, inviting his love. "My dearest," he whispered to himself.

Suddenly, jolted by the reality of the battle before him, he instantly refocused upon the spectacle of conflict and on the profound responsibility that was his, alone, to shoulder. For all to see, he raised his gloveless hand in a flamboyant manner, holding it aloft before thrusting it forwards several times – his urgent signal for Borthwick to begin firing at once.

In those gaps between the two central divisions and the left wing, the Scottish crews attending each gun were prepared, though not as they had been on Flodden where the cannon were entrenched and sighted, secure in their wooden frames. On Branxton Hill's northern slope, there had been insufficient time to set them up correctly. As a result, the first salvoes proved useless, the missiles flying too high, way overhead of their targets. The recoil also dislodged the guns from their moorings and frantic crews were compelled to realign them after each explosion, wasting precious time as they strained with the weight.

In response, the English field cannon had begun firing uphill, an operation that proved more favourable from below in assessing angle and range. Being lighter, the guns were also easier to handle and align. Consequently, it wasn't long before their artillery teams displayed skills that were more practical and efficient than their opponents', recording direct hits upon the Scottish gunners.

As the artillery battle raged, the foot soldiers on both sides stood raw-nerved and awe-struck, transfixed by the tumultuous noise and sheer terror of standing in the open, vulnerable and helpless against weapons that were at least three arrow-shots' distance from them. No one was immune. When the ground shuddered, even the brave did too.

It was soon evident that the up-slope bouncing of the smaller English cannon balls, reaping through the Scottish ordnance, was causing wholescale havoc and mayhem amongst gunners and crewmen. Howling in pain, those men who were smashed or maimed tumbled to the ground, bowled over like skittles. In comparison, the Scottish siege guns' return fire was ponderous, and only a few achieved near strikes. On the brow of Branxton Hill, aiming downwards, barrel elevation was difficult to gauge and slow to adjust. Moreover, any cannon balls that crashed onto the lower, facing slope of Piper's Hill plunged into the ground rather than skip over the surface, thus limiting their destructive harm.

Encouraged by their rate of success, the English teams worked tirelessly, firing three times more quickly than the Scots managed. While the English gun-master, Appleyard, bawled orders enthusiastically, Borthwick ranted at his artillery's failing. "Load faster. Alter your aim!" he screamed, waving his arms in exasperation. "For God's sake, fire upon them!" At the back of his mind he rued the fact that he had been denied permission by King James to shoot earlier, for the outcome might then have been so very different. Before his eyes, his prized cannon were being out-fought and, to his dismay, terrified crewmen amidst the wreckage began to run from their bays in a frantic dash for survival.

Grieved at the sight of his magnificent guns damaged or abandoned, King James was appalled to witness the English artillery beginning to target his own soldiers' tight pike formations. A sense of calamity furnaced his thoughts and his face turned scarlet. Ironically, the chaos and carnage that he had envisaged developing among the English ranks had unexpectedly turned on his own. Utterly exposed and defenceless against this long-distance barrage, he knew that he had no other option but to attack immediately, much earlier than planned. While the shooting continued, he shouted orders for the left vanguard to move downhill first, employing the pike assault strategy in which the French had instructed his soldiers.

Between explosions, a fanfare of trumpets was heard. Home's Borderers lowered their pikes and with their shields before them, advanced at pace, knitted together firmly in their square formations, flanked on either side by Huntly's wild looking Highlanders armed with bows and two-handed claymore swords. Down below, Edmund Howard's outnumbered English right division braced itself apprehensively at the terrifying sight of this fast approaching horde of warriors.

To the consternation of their young commander, even before the two forces met, sections of frightened Englishmen turned and ran, ignoring the rallying calls screamed at them by comrades and officers alike. Many of the fugitives, already disheartened by their transfer from their own company when reorganised earlier in the valley, were more than ready to abandon their fight against what seemed an overwhelming attack.

At the front, the English longbowmen attempted first to impede the Scots' approach but to no avail. Protected by an improved armour and firm discipline, Home's division, unchecked, slowed down only slightly to cross the small stream at the foot of the hill, where Archie Tait's body lay. Passing over the muddy strip, onto firmer, more level ground, they quickly regained their charge towards a flimsy-looking English defence, tremulously clutching their bills.

The collision proved catastrophic for Edmund Howard's soldiers. The shorter halberds were no match against the jagged, impenetrable wall of pikes crashing into them. English front men, without the satisfaction of a single blow, were driven through, and the onslaught proceeded to stampede forward like a tempest, unstoppable and deadly, starkly demonstrating the long spears' famed, lethal use.

Resistance was suicidally brave. Disgusted by many of his men's desertion, Thomas Venables led his troop of Cheshiremen into the fray and, fighting for their honour, were soon overcome and bludgeoned to the ground. The Macclesfield unit, led by Sir Christopher Savage, struggled to hold its position. Assaulted on one side by the Highlanders' swords and arrows, and by the thrusting pikemen before them, they were rapidly overwhelmed – speared, gashed and ripped apart by a torrent of violent blows.

Not far from them, Robert Foulsehurst, leading by example, courageously exhorted his dwindling company to follow him in an offensive rally towards Home's flag, only to find themselves surrounded by blood-crazed Scottish Border men who battered and hacked them down with relish.

As soon as the English lines were bloodily splintered and torn, the Scottish pike columns were themselves forced to split up into several factions, and throwing their long spears aside, were reduced to hand-to-hand fighting. Attacking deeper into the English ranks with swords flailing, a band of Teviotdale soldiers, including the Taits, Youngs and Burns, came face to face with a colony of robust fighters from Redesdale. In the savagery of this engagement, the Milburn and Charlton family men fought courageously in defence of Edmund Howard's standard. Briefly, the Northumbrians pressed the opposition with bills cutting and chopping, and Seth Milburn and some of his kin were able to cleave their way forward, toppling those before them.

Seth, splattered with the blood of others, knocked another Scot over and was about to strike him dead on the ground when he saw the boy's blank face. He grabbed young Ewan Burn by the arm, yanked him to his feet and pushed him aside. "Run lad! Flee the field," Seth rasped.

Continuing to attack, hurling themselves at the enemy, the English fighters rapidly found themselves faced by more and more Scots whose weight of numbers halted their advance and drove them back. Davie Charlton lost half his head from a mighty Highlander's sword. Black Bob Milburn was speared in the gut and his brother, Samuel of Hepple Linn, sword arm already severed, was whipped off his feet and his chest caved in by an axe.

Seth, his brother Dick, his uncle Lance, and brother-in-law Mossy Charlton gave ground, their lungs heaving for breath. Sitting on the grass with blood spurting from his left thigh, Harry Milburn from Otterburn waved desperately at Lance who was nearest to him. Amid the howling and wailing of the wounded and dying from both sides, he called out for Lance's aid. Lance turned his head and for an instant their eyes met. "Help me," mouthed Harry. "Help me." Lance paused, then deliberately spat on the ground and retreated.

44

After his distress at his cannon's failure, King James was thrilled now by his left wing's seeming rout of the English right. Having already ordered Crawford, Errol and Montrose to descend, he readied his own centre-right division to move downhill in succession. His heart boomed with nervous exhilaration. Now the time had come to lead his nation to the victory of his gold-gilded dream. He focused his mind upon the challenge and filled his chest with a long, slow breath, willing himself to fight for glory.

At the front of each Scottish square or schiltron, the more heavily armoured soldiers – the nobility, knights, and men-at-arms – formed an offensive arrowhead to breach the enemy's line. With King James placed in the tip of this wedge, his standard bearer and household guards about him, he lowered his helmet's face guard and commenced the downward march to confront the Earl of Surrey's own left-centre army.

What the two Scottish central divisions did not anticipate was the slippery drop of the hill below them, far steeper than that which Home and Huntly's men had faced. Moving carefully to maintain their shape, the pike formations, still enduring deadly artillery fire, had to slow their approach, thereby losing the decisiveness of their action. Even more of a hindrance, they found the ditch of the small stream at the bottom of the slope wider and deeper than that which the left wing had crossed, upfield. Saturated by two weeks' perpetual rain, the ground in the dip was sodden and as the first troops lumbered across it, the earth was quickly ploughed up, turning it into a quagmire that severely disrupted their formations' crossing. Most tellingly, unlike Home's rapid advance, the acceleration of their pike attack had essentially lost its initial momentum, decreasing its vital thrust.

To attempt to counter both Scottish attacks, the admiral and Surrey had sent their bowmen down, closer to the hollow, to hail arrows into the oncoming ranks. Because of the previous weeks' wet weather, the vibrancy of their bows to power the arrows was diminished and they pierced the armour of very few men. They did, however, make it hazardous for the Scots as they struggled to reorder their charge up the short incline towards the two main English divisions – a climb that had not been appreciated when looking down from the summit of Branxton Hill.

****

Meanwhile, the situation to the west, on flatter ground, was becoming dire for Edmund Howard's outnumbered soldiers. Beaten back with horrendous losses, his remaining force faced total defeat. He himself was seen as a valuable capture for ransom and a contingent of Home's Borderers was slaying a bloody path towards him. Among his defenders, Straughen fought with fury, aiding Howard's personal guards to repel

Scottish attempts to snatch their leader. In one fray, Edmund was knocked over, but he adroitly rolled back up onto his feet and slashed wildly at his assailants, wounding two and killing one.

It was at this point – learning of the emergency – that Surrey, from his carriage, committed Lord Dacre's cavalry reserve to ride to his son's aid. The news of his army's plight on the right wing, and of Stanley's continuing absence on the battlefield's left, disturbed him greatly and did not bode well for the oncoming fight against the king's most powerful division. The lines on the old general's face scored deeper and he began to feel alarm jabbing at his resolve. "God give us strength and protect us," he uttered.

Charging into battle, Dacre's two thousand Border riders set about their counterparts with hateful, craving vengeance. In close combat, the Scots had cast aside their unwieldy pikes. This enabled Dacre's lancers to drive into them using their spears and crossbows to break through enemy groups, maiming or killing many in their way.

Spotting the young commander's beleaguered group struggling desperately to reach the protection of the Lord Admiral's division, Heron and his party of riders aimed their horses across the field to enter young Howard's defence. Attacking from the side, the riding troopers barged into the Scots, lunging their spears to break through. As soon as the enemy's clustered numbers slowed them down, Heron and his followers leapt to the ground and continued to fight on foot in a fierce, ruthless and bloody encounter, screams of agony and hurt doused by the sizzling rain.

Not that far from them, in another affray, the Milburns and the Charltons were fighting for their lives against a unit of Scotsmen relentlessly teeming forward. Fending off two, Seth Milburn tripped on a dead body and fell on his back. Seizing his chance, one of the two leaped forward raising his sword. Suddenly, the other Scot grabbed his partner's arm to prevent the blow. "No!" shouted Jock Burn. He allowed Seth to scramble onto his feet. "You saved m' laddie. Back away!" he bellowed.

Numb-faced in disbelief, Seth quickly retreated into the fold of his own men to continue the fight. Fortunately for them, some of Dacre's horsemen joined the melee, forcing the Scots to defend, enabling Seth and his band to regroup and stand firm.

45

At the end of a short but intense period of slaughter, Dacre's intervention succeeded in stemming the massacre and Home and Huntly's soldiers suffered increased loss as a consequence. Among the white surcoated bodies, scattered like May blossom across the ground, a substantial number of Scottish Borderers and Highlanders had fallen too, slain by bill, spear, sword or crossbow. Throughout the gruesome action, underpinning the jarring din of combat, a strange and macabre chorus of cries rose from the crawling wounded and dying, while others lay silent, stunned with pain, staring hazily at the earth or sky.

In disarray, the conflict on this side of the field dwindled. Physically exhausted, drained emotionally by the fury of killing, the fighting gradually ceased and soldiers pulled back, panting to regain their breath whilst taking stock of the situation.

That of Edmund Howard's infantry which had not been scythed down, or driven off, stood in sorrowful batches across the field's northern edge alongside Dacre's cavalry, facing the Scottish host that otherwise claimed most of the area. And in the pause, the Borderers' instinct for gain took hold and the Scots, by measure of their success, began to scour and plunder, robbing the dead of weapons, clothes, boots, and any other personal item they could find, such as jewellery or keepsakes. Watching helplessly, the English soldiers stood like mere spectators, doleful and glum-faced, dejected by loss.

Aware that the press of engagement had worn itself out, leaders signalled for horns to be blown, and soldiers from both sides withdrew further apart and gathered to their own, rain-heavy flags which drooped and swayed in the blustery winds. It was here, now, that the scale of casualties could be reckoned, from the common man to the full-armoured noble. Although the English right wing had not been wholly defeated, in terms of soldiers slain, the Scots were undoubtedly triumphant.

Significantly, Edmund Howard's standard had been captured but he had survived, due in part to his own valour and that of his retainers plus men like Straughen and later, Heron, who in a frantic skirmish had also been injured, his upper left arm gashed and bloody. Like so many who never saw the men who struck them, he'd been caught blind by an assailant from the side. Although wounded, he had instinctively swung round with his sword in his right hand and almost decapitated his attacker. Supported by his loyal henchmen, he had continued to ward off the threat to the younger Howard and helped usher him towards the admiral's fighting troops that were stretched down slope from Piper's Hill.

In the mayhem of this rescue, Foxy Tom Dunne and his twin brother Rob, standing their ground, became isolated, their plight unheeded, and were savaged by a swarm of Scottish fighters who hewed them down – the twins dying as they were born, together.

46

Here, on the gentle southern slope of Piper's Hill, the conflict was more balanced. When the reorganised pike columns attempted a rush up the ascent into the English lines, Bulmer's Durham archers scurried away from the front allowing the admiral's heavily armoured professionals, halberds flailing, to counter the Scots' lunge. Hampered by the terrain and dogged English resistance, the run of pikes was considerably weakened and their use no longer devastating.

Stride after stride, the Scottish offence was shortened to mere steps, eventually slowing to a halt. Parrying the long spears, the admiral's bill-men were now able to splinter the poles, shearing off their points. Finding themselves thrust forward by the weight of soldiers cramming up behind them, the well-armoured Scottish front ranks, led by the three earls, were compelled to cast down their useless shafts and fight on with swords against the longer bills. Reeling against the vicious slashing and gouging of the more potent weapon, Scottish casualties increased dramatically.

In the murderous clash, the armoured earls and knights of Scotland showed incredible courage. But swords and bravery were not enough against the lethal bill-hook, which cut and thrust and axed them to the ground. In hand-to-hand fighting, the admiral's trained soldiers worked in gangs of three or four and combined to target individual nobles, slicing and hooking their legs to send them crashing. Once downed and their movement restricted by weight of armour, they were easily dispatched.

Despite their losses, the Scottish square division continued to squeeze forward, making little headway but intent on killing and breaking through the linear defence employed by the enemy. This progress, however, served to envelop them from the front and sides as the English overlap closed round, wrapping them into a tighter, ferocious and unmanageable struggle.

****

By this time, the king's grander division, having squelched and laboured through the stream's marshy bottom and prevailed through the arrows, began its surge up the short incline with renewed passion. James's nobles and knights, inspired by their leader's zest, were initially successful. The impact of their pike charge bent the English line backwards and, for a short while, their aggressive bulk of thousands seemed likely to smash through.

Yet, despite the English formation buckling and backing off, the hardy English bill-men, mainly from South Yorkshire, did not lose control, and their stout resistance gradually saw the pike attack slacken and then grind to a halt. At a standstill, the Scottish pikes now proved cumbersome and, as had happened with those pikes on their left – under the earls' command, the bills swiftly rendered them useless. Casting their pikes aside, the intrepid Scots drew their swords and fought on in desperation behind their bold, impulsive king, intent on progress. And in the clatter of steel and screech of wrath, men lunged towards levels of insane cruelty, ensnared by a whirlwind of bloodshed and murder.

****

Meanwhile, on the English right, where the first of the battles had earlier petered out, Lord Home was clearly aware that his troops had all but won and he strode forward, ringed with guards, to glare towards Dacre, who, seated at the head of his riders, had reassembled to keep watch from a distance. The rivalry between these two Border lords was renowned. In the brief confrontation, no attempt was made to communicate, other than a stern, hostile stare; a fixed regard that conveyed a simple, unspoken message: enough of it.

Turning about, Home led his men back across the ground strewn mainly with English dead and spoke with Huntly of withdrawal. The Highland chief shook his head, wishing their regiments to continue, entering the battle to the right of them in support of the earls – Crawford, Errol and Montrose. "Surely 'tis right, my noble lord, if aid is needed we be at their side?" appealed Huntly.

A dubious Lord Home raised his head to survey his massed soldiers clutching their booty. Many squatted or sat upon the ground, resting and recovering from their ordeal, their strength spent, their mood reflective, and released from the fires of violence that had burned within. As well as the loss of many good and ordinary men, he considered the landowners from his own and other leading Border families that had been killed, along with four Highland chieftains. Bitterly, he remembered, too, his humiliation by Sir William Bulmer's archers at Milfield, a month before, where he'd lost several hundred men. He scanned the field of slaughtered soldiers where his troops had gained supremacy, and perceived that the dead and dying were already a worthy tribute to the king's great cause and his inevitable victory. What more, he concluded, could he owe his master, than this?

Alexander, Lord Home drew a long breath before announcing his decision. "My good Earl of Huntly, have our men not given all? See before you," he gestured with a sweep of his hands. "Clearly we've played our part and won. I say let the rest do as well," he asserted, then gave orders for his contingent to retreat up the hill to collect their horses, leaving the carnage of battle behind them.

Huntly, perplexed, but unable to argue with the senior commander whose Border fighters were in the majority, instructed his Highland troops to withdraw accordingly.

The watching English stared in disbelief. Dry-mouthed, a sense of relief swelled their hearts. Eyes closed, many gave silent thanks for God's mercy. Others simply stood motionless, bewildered by the raw picture of killing and death, and the miracle of their survival.

Once the departed Scots had moved out of range, posing no further threat, Lord Dacre seized the opportunity with energy, ordering his full complement of riders, now fewer than seventeen hundred, to follow himself and Heron towards the battle raging to their left. Here, the rugged aggression of the admiral's bill-men was now dominant and they, at last, were storming the Scottish ranks whose swords and axes were outmatched by the shearing, murderous halberds. Absorbing the scene as they approached it, Thomas Dacre gladly unleashed his cavalry upon the failing enemy.

47

Had Home and Huntly's thousands given the three Scottish earls their support, attacking from the flank, the situation might have been very different, certainly for a time, tilting the outcome in favour of the Scots. Instead, the Scottish lords and knights fronting their division faced a ruthless onslaught by the admiral's tough, experienced soldiers. In their bold but futile attempt to lead by example at the front, the earls of Crawford, Errol and Montrose were brutally assaulted, spiked and hacked to death, along with a score of other nobles from their family clans.

As the front lines of the Scottish schiltron were successively demolished, confusion and disarray in the tight middle and rear ranks resulted in many terrified levies, mostly poor farm labourers, attempting to run from the spiral of butchery aiming towards them. For a number of these soldiers, this proved an escape that ended in death at the hands of archers and those of Dacre's lancers who, at the smell of blood, gave chase on horseback, like a pack of killer hounds.

****

Informed of his younger son's survival, Surrey clasped his hands in grateful prayer. His mind brightened further when he learned from his aide, Simmons, of the English left wing's approach into Crookham. Inspired by this news, the general hastily sent his Northumbrian messenger back to the village to inform Lord Stanley of the Highlanders' position – waiting on the east side of Branxton Hill, and for him to consider ways to challenge them. He was encouraged, too, by what he heard and saw of the admiral's encounter, but was apprehensive for his own division, which was robustly withstanding the onslaught of the king's massive, fiendish attack.

Unlike the earl – the English leader, who received constant reports of the situation and was able to judge and direct operations from a relatively safe vantage point, the Scottish king, himself immersed in fighting, was unable to view matters objectively and thus deliver orders that were essential to his army's cause. Of course, this miscalculation was the very shortcoming Angus and others predicted, but which King James, perversely, refused to accept.

Stubborn or short-sighted, the Scottish king had also failed to appoint a second-in-charge to deputise for him in the emergency of war. As a result, Bothwell, commanding the reserve, and Lennox and Argyll with their Highland division, were left uncertain with no clear instructions as to how and when they should enter the battle. While the fighting raged below, they stood dumbfounded, watching from on high, exposed only to the wind and rain and the gloom of early evening.

Despite their fury, the king's front wave of attack made little progress as the English troops performed staunchly, able to contain it. Although edging backwards, the disciplined English lines remained resolute against the splendidly armoured wedge of Scotland's finest men. James and his nobles were indomitable, swords swinging, lashing and cutting with sustained power at the obstinate English defence. Yet the bill-men stayed fast, with fresh fighters replacing those who fell or dropped back exhausted, thereby able to hold their walled formation; every man straining in hope that the Scottish attack would eventually tire and its resolve begin to wilt.

From his carriage, set on raised ground to the south of Branxton village behind his army, the veteran Surrey perceived the movement of Bothwell's reserve commencing to advance down hill to join the battle. Decisively, he sent Simmons with an immediate message to his son, the admiral, demanding that he spare soldiers from his winning regiments to join them in their fight against the king's larger division.

Surrey's second ploy was to have trumpets blown, signalling to his captains for the central lines to drop back as earlier planned, drawing the king's men forward into a pocket where they could be overlapped and attacked from both sides as well as at the head. Lastly, he sent orders to Dacre that he wanted Heron to lead a mounted foray downslope to violently distract and disrupt Bothwell's reserve force as it scrambled across the ditch in the marshy hollow. For on no account did he, the earl, want Bothwell's columns coming alongside the king's division, creating another front.

Summoning Heron aside, Lord Dacre hurriedly gave him the order. Heron's wounded upper-left arm was tightly bandaged but strong enough to clutch his shield. Dacre glanced at the bloodstained wrapping. "We depend upon you," he cried above the battle's din. Undaunted, Heron accepted the challenge and within minutes a cavalry troop of over three hundred riders armed with shields, crossbows, lances and swords was withdrawn from the final stages of what was now a near massacre of the Scots' left-centre division.

At a gallop, Heron's unit circled about from Piper's Hill and with Straughen as his second, he led the charge past the sea of fighting ranks, over a small brow and swooped down to the stream hollow, across which Bothwell's foremost pikemen were already staggering.

Commanding his crossbowmen into a facing line, they quickly fired off their bolts into the crowded morass then wheeled away. Following them, Heron immediately drove the rest of his spear-carrying riders into a daring, curving raid, splitting through the horrified Scots before they had time to position themselves. Though this manoeuvre could not be sustained as more and more of Bothwell's three thousand soldiers slogged through the bog, it served to unnerve them. Recognised by Scottish levies from the Border areas, Heron's dreaded name was echoed in alarm. Having been detached on the hilltop from the reality of the battle, Bothwell's troops now entered the scene of violence with hearts already jittery and their morale visibly shaken.

Harassed by Heron's horsed bowmen and by their lance-stabbing forays, the Scottish reserve strained up the slight slope in an attempt to join the king's rear columns. What they saw before them was utter turmoil and panic.

Assailed by English bill-men on all sides, the lower orders of the king's division were fast losing co-ordination and their ranks were clearly disintegrating as men, like reaped grass, fell about them, howling in agony, soaked in blood. Assisted by more and more of Dacre's Border cavalry galloping over to offer support, plus a stream of the admiral's foot-soldiers crossing the field to increase the attack on the Scottish flank, Surrey's lines were visibly strengthened to the point that they were more than capable of blunting the fierce advance of the king's men.

Even though the great battle here seemed to be balanced now more in England's favour, the old Commander-in-Chief was still worried by the Highlanders' looming presence on the east of the hill. Without Stanley's protection, they could quite easily launch an attack in support of King

James and swing the battle back his way.

Lips and eyes pinched shut, as if in pain, Surrey prayed desperately that fortune remained with him, and that circumstance would prove to be his blessed ally.

48

The Northumbrian rider that Surrey had earlier sent from the battlefield to inform Lord Stanley of the Highlanders' position was no less a figure than Adam Weatherburn of Ewart, one of Heron's main associates. As a local man his close knowledge of the terrain, Surrey believed, could prove useful to Stanley in his final approach to the battle.

For a commoner, Badger Weatherburn was an articulate man, as Surrey had discovered the evening before the English had left Wooler, when he'd made his rounds, inspecting the troops, and had spoken with him. Being one of Heron's most wanted men, he wittily dared to thank the old earl for not having hanged them all when they'd handed themselves over.

"If we lose the battle and you're still alive, I may have to," jested the earl.

"If it be a battle t' lose, not a battle t' win, then w' must not be the side t' lose, my lord," cackled Weatherburn in response, his hazel-coloured eyes beaming. The spontaneous, quirky reply impressed Surrey and he made a point of remembering the man, selecting him to be one of his messengers before the fighting started.

At the edge of Crookham village, a mile to the east of Branxton, Weatherburn was stopped and identified by Lancaster guards, and then escorted to meet Lord Stanley, to deliver Surrey's message. His red neckerchief indicated his allegiance to Heron.

Before speaking, Weatherburn removed his helmet to scratch his head. A gloss of sweat watered his forehead. Those around him noticed his damp, rusty hair parted by a natural, grey streak. "My Lord Surrey asks you t' make haste and consider the Scottish Highlanders still on the hill. They've no pikes like the others and seem in a quandary as to when the' should join the battle."

"How goes the battle?" demanded Stanley, with a measured look at this chirpy character before him.

"It leans towards us, but the earl fears it could easy shift away without your help. He needs you t' come quickly!" urged Weatherburn.

Stanley, astutely, had already sent scouts ahead and knew as much. "Perhaps some of us can surprise the Highlanders by going round that way, behind them." He pointed to the hill to the left beyond the burn. "Is it possible to remain out of sight until we get close to them?"

Weatherburn gazed towards the mossy hill on the south side of Crookham Dene. He nodded. "It's known as Pace Hill, m' lord. And further up on the moor the's more trees t' hide us from them. But the'll be no reason t' go there if the Scots have left the hill. You'll need to fix them there somehow with what's happenin' below," he advised, shrewdly.

High cheek-boned with a broad nose, a pugnacious looking Stanley studied the individual before him. He reflected that Surrey always seemed to choose able men to do his work. For a coarse-looking rogue, Weatherburn was clearly sharp-minded and crafty, as well as amiable.

Abruptly, setting his plans into motion, Stanley turned his horse and once more briefed his nobles – Sir William Molyneux, Sir Thomas Gerrard, Sir Henry Kighley and two younger officers, relatives from his Lancashire family. The scheme had already been defined, so the two junior officers quickly set about their task of leading over five hundred men along the small valley road, on the south side of the morass stretching along the Pallinsburn, to Branxton. Following their departure, the remaining two and a half thousand troops, including Stanley's famed archers, began to move towards the facing hill. At the front of this column rode Lord Edward Stanley, with his guide, Weatherburn, directing their path.

On the eastern forward slope of Branxton Hill the two Scottish commanders, the earls Lennox and Argyll, were able to gather from the action they observed below them that the English army had not been swept away as predicted, but was strongly opposing King James's advance and gradually hemming in his division on both sides.

The longer the Highlanders awaited orders from the field, their dilemma grew. Dangling on the hillside in the streaming rain and wind, their men's willingness for warfare was dimming fast. Being clansmen from the far north, their loyalty to an ambitious king was secondary to their allegiance to their own chieftains. Many had been absent from home for more than a month and their hearts pined to return. Disenchanted by their non-participation and the presence of a small, foreign contingent of French soldiers assigned with them, the attitude in the ranks was turning more careless and dispirited.

The two earls, Matthew Stewart and Archibald Campbell, were of the same opinion that they must act soon, leading a charge diagonally downhill into the left flank of the English and to the relief of King James's force. The French Knight, Count d'Aussi, who had ridden across to join them when Bothwell's reserve moved down the hill, attempted to dissuade them, believing it might, at this stage, entangle the king's division rather than free it. He argued, diplomatically, that to wrest control from the hand of the king would be a violation of duty.

"From the front line he cannot perceive what we see already. I say we attack now!" countered Lennox, exasperation burning in his voice.

"Count d'Aussi," entreated Argyll, "our men are rapidly losing interest. Without rage in their veins our Highlanders do not fight heartily. I say we delay no further."

Count d'Aussi, small, slim, aristocratic in manner, pondered a reply to these brash, bearded chiefs. He surveyed the action again and his eyes slid towards movement on the empty field to the east of the conflict below them. The earls saw his expression change and they directly followed his gaze downhill. "I think you should reconsider your decision, noble lords," observed the Frenchman politely, though a touch scathing as Stanley's banners rose out of the little valley and a slow procession of English soldiers filed forwards in preparation to fight them.

A mumbling crept through the Highlanders' division. There was something uncanny about the way the opposing English force deliberately and methodically formed their lines, trickling over the low ridge into view, unhurried, a group at a time. The murmuring faded as the Highlanders watched and waited, spellbound by the slow unfurling of the enemy over the crest below, taking up their battle positions.

Someone in the ranks felt the need to break their silence. A dagger or sword handle began to beat a wooden shield. Others joined in and the beating escalated into a fierce, pounding rhythm accompanied by Gaelic war cries.

The French count protested. The pike columns had been trained to attack in concentrated silence, as the Swiss method dictated. Although the Highlanders were armed with broadswords, spears and axes rather than pikes, d'Aussi was irritated by their clamour. Lennox turned on him to remonstrate. "It is our way. We raise our voices to stoke hatred and rage. We cannot fight like muzzled wolves. To tie their tongues you may as well ask our men to fight with one hand held behind their backs. It is, Your Excellency, the way of the Highlanders and even we, their leaders, dare not suppress it!"

In the din of drumming shields, they heard nothing of the English soldiers stalking forward through the trees to their right, or the body of archers creeping closer over the shoulder of the hill to their rear, which was still misted by wraiths of lingering smoke from Flodden's rubbish fires. After the slippery scramble up Pace Hill where many of his men had removed their shoes to gain a better grip, Stanley's company had followed Crookham Dene up onto the moor from where they sneaked towards the Highlanders' stand. With the Scots' attention riveted to the sustained deployment of the English opposition below, Stanley signalled for his skilled archers to halt and raise their longbows. Made of finest yew and protected daily from dampness, their potency had been preserved by master bowmen.

Weatherburn watched the first blizzard of arrows gush through the air hitting their targets – the unprotected backs of Highlanders. At once, warring howls became shrieks of pain and their threatening roars turned into cries of agony as the pointed shafts pierced skin and flesh. The Scottish ranks turned in bewilderment and were immediately struck by a second avalanche of arrows. Wearing less armour than other Scottish divisions, stricken clansmen collapsed and tumbled, or staggered off clutching wounds. For the brave who gathered themselves to counter-attack the English archers, the Highlanders' ragged lines were then startled by waves of Stanley's soldiers brandishing bills, running out of the nearby wood and charging towards them.

Terrorised by the ambush and the number of casualties dropping amongst them, a host of frenzied Scots ran off to escape the clouds of fresh arrows descending upon them before the bill-men's charge was met. Their flight induced panic in others and despite the urgent rants of their leaders and chiefs to stay and fight, increasing numbers left their ranks, bolting off downhill.

As Stanley's charging infantry, directed by Molyneux, Gerrard and Kighley plunged into the flank of the depleted Scots, the two earls and their noblemen put up a strenuous fight. Desperate to rally their clansmen, they found themselves driven backwards by the Lancashire and Cheshire soldiers wading in with their bill-hooks flailing, swiping, carving and gouging all before them. Despite their courage, the Scots' shorter swords, axes and knives proved inferior when up against the daunting bill-hook, wielded in the hands of skilled, furious English soldiers.

The underclass may have chosen to run but not the men of status and stature. Bludgeoned backwards, Lennox, Argyll, Caithness, Darnley and clan headmen fought until they were ruthlessly chopped down, along with the gentry and loyal family members that refused to flee. Nearby, Count d'Aussi and half of his French platoon were knocked over and slain as well, much to the glee of English victors, grabbing what plunder they could easily carry from the sunken enemy.

Exhilarated by their tremendous, devastating success, Stanley's men either stayed to finish off the remaining huddles of doomed Scotsmen, prepared to fight to the death, or went in chase of those who dashed away, fleeing past the slaughter-ground below towards Scotland. Among the fugitives aiming to reach the Border river were about twenty French soldiers who followed a large band of Scots, hoping that they would lead them to safety. The Highlanders, however, seeking revenge for their misfortune, later rounded on the foreigners they despised and, savagely, butchered them all before crossing the ford into Coldstream.

Having accomplished an amazingly short but remarkable victory, a proud Lord Stanley laid a gloved hand on Weatherburn's shoulder. "Praise God that we have won!" he cried, his eyes wild with jubilation.

Weatherburn, gloating, held up the French count's exquisitely pearled sword. "I've been praising Him since I was born, my lord, for the gifts He provides me."

Stanley chortled, smacking Weatherburn's shoulder in delight. Then he gave orders to his officers to reassemble as much of his division as possible, including the decoy unit that had been shrewdly deployed on the field below. He was keenly aware that it was imperative now for his men to move on quickly, angling down the hillside to support Surrey's fight against the struggling might of King James's force. Looking up at the sky, he calculated that there was hardly an hour of light left to end the day.

49

Embroiled in frontline attack, King James was too immersed in action to see the reality of the situation. He assumed that his left wing, having crushed the English right, would assist the three earls against the admiral's troops. He'd heard it shouted that Bothwell's reserve had come down to add support but had no idea of how they fared. He also anticipated that the broadsword-wielding Highlanders on the right would descend in time to reinforce his flank.

In truth, he knew nothing of Home's retreat or the rout of his

Highlanders on the right wing under Lennox and Argyll. What he was learning, more surely, was that the English resistance had barred his assault and each time it seemed that their defensive line might splinter, others stepped forward to close the gaps, fighting ferociously, their opposition indefatigable and unyielding.

Amidst the frenzied killing, King James could only consider the enemy he faced, his reactions spontaneous, as though swatting flies. Fighting with his nobles and men-at-arms, the lust to kill, to destroy those standing in his way, was all-consuming. Enticed by the hideous glare of the enemy, their worthless beings blocking his pathway to glory – to the pinnacle of triumph and exaltation – his passion drove his company on, forging ahead, unaware of the ranks disintegrating behind as the English assault continued to shatter them from all sides: Dacre's Border men, Heron's troopers, the admiral's professionals, Constable and Bulmer's soldiers from Yorkshire, Durham and Northumberland, Stanley's units from Lancashire and Cheshire, and even Edmund Howard's remnants from his vanquished division – each of them striving towards the absolute destruction of the king's bold but withering force.

Worn out by the strain of physical violence, the weight of their armour and brandishing of weapons, King James and his squad paused to regain their breath, gulping air, a look of exhaustion upon their faces. The English too, keen for respite, stood back, panting, chests heaving, faces wet with sweat and rain.

In the brief interlude, James took account of his advance and his narrow, blinkered awareness suddenly flooded open, recognising the dreadful slaughter about him, mostly of Scots, including his earls of Morton and Rothes, his lords, Herries, Maxwell and Borthwick, many of his household knights and guards, dear friends and, closest of all, his son, the Archbishop. He'd led the strongest fist of his Scottish army into battle and it was now crumbling about him. Woefully, he turned his head and was confounded by the burden of his dead companions, his countrymen, victims of the English bill – the wrathful weapon that had thrashed and sliced open his sworded braves.

He stared in disbelief upon the horror of his lost men, the dead and the whining and tortured wounded crawling helplessly over one another. His sense told him bluntly, like a scream, that his army's power was almost perished. He gazed beyond, grappling with the image of defeat, the scorn of those critics and sceptics that had haunted and plagued him nightly: his murdered father, his wife Queen Margaret, the Earl of Angus, Bishop Elphinstone and, eerily, the smiling Earl of Surrey!

With his face-guard raised to allow him to breathe more easily, King James stared ahead, eyes smarting, when he spotted him – Surrey, the veteran earl standing in his open carriage and looking towards him. James tensed, holding his breath; the English general, no more than thirty strides away, was there before him, within reach. James raised his sword in recognition. Surrey appeared to respond, raising both arms, as Lady Heron had done, inviting him to come closer.

The Scottish king ground his teeth, a single thought bursting within him: If he could reach the old leader and slay him, the battle would not be lost! With the Earl of Surrey dead, his severed head held aloft for all to see, the English forces, uprooted by his loss, would instantly wilt, prompting James's men to revive their energy and ambition. Together, with their king, their renewed morale would restore a strength and desire to fight harder, to persevere, and earn a just and stunning victory.

Reflecting upon the gesture that Surrey appeared to have made, the king fleetingly perceived again the vision of his lovely Lady Elizabeth, and her beckoning. Snatching her brooch from his sleeve, he began to shout at his followers. "For God and country, once more exalt yourselves to fight." He pointed his sword towards the English general. "We have him before us. Victory is nigh!" he roared. For safekeeping, he thrust the brooch into his mouth and, in haste, forgetting to drop his face-guard, he surged forward again, sword lashing out to carve a route through the opposing English soldiers towards their Commander-in-Chief. Entranced by this single aim of hope and redemption, he felt tears of joy.

They had gained little ground when Sir Adam Foreman, his standard bearer, was hacked down, immediately followed by the killing of the Earl of Cassillis, then the lords, Innermeath and Semphill, along with others sworn by oath at Boroughmoor, near Edinburgh, to protect and serve their king.

Blinded by his doomed vision, King James vented his grief with a final sword-swinging surge, fatally wounding two more of the enemy obstructing his way before he felt a searing burn across his left wrist. He glanced down at his gloved hand dangling from strings of skin and sinew. His unprotected mouth gaped open in pain and an arrow entered, boring through his neck. He spluttered and the brooch was coughed out; still clutching his sword, he instinctively bent down to retrieve it from the mud but his severed hand would not respond. Aghast, he numbly raised his head and a bill-hook's blade spliced his face apart. He crashed over. Prostrate in the dirt, his last gaze floated in a pool of his own blood. A cold throbbing crawled down his spine and in the final tick of consciousness he was minutely aware that the brooch, like Surrey, was unattainable.

In the packed scrum of fighting, his fall was passed over as individuals around him, wholly absorbed in their own deliverance, died too. Bodies stumbled and staggered and sprawled about him, his part now over, his role ended, simply another victim, another corpse; one more to add to the shocking list.

50

Across the blood-spilled field as evening was darkening, the fighting continued at random, in skirmishes here and there. Small companies of gallant Scotsmen who refused to run continued to oppose the overpowering numbers of English troops wielding their bills, swords, spears and bows. Those who tried to surrender were shown no mercy, unless of high birth and worthy of ransom. Among the few snatched were such notables as Sir John Foreman and Sir William Scott of Balwearie. A great many from the terrified ranks that fled the field were pursued, while more and more English soldiers on the site seized the opportunity to rob from the Scottish dead, as well as from their own countrymen. Entangled bodies were pulled clear of one another, stripped of their garments and weapons and left pathetically naked and degraded on the ground. Any Scotsmen crying and groaning, as they lay injured, were summarily executed without pity and they, too, fleeced of their possessions.

* * * *

Before daylight had disappeared completely, a section of Dacre's Border men, led by Heron, was ordered up the hill by Surrey to capture the prized Scottish artillery. There, they stole the unattended horses that the Scots had left behind before the battle. Lord Home's Borderers, of course, before they'd retreated had already taken their share. Heron and his band were also instructed by Dacre to seek out any further resistance.

Including reinforcement, Bastard Heron led about five hundred men on a short ride westward to locate where Home's men might possibly have reassembled, but there was no sight of them in the semi-dark. Later, Heron heard from his scouts that they were stationed at the fords over the Tweed and at routes through the hills, escorting the thousands of Scottish fugitives crossing the Border who sought the sanctuary of their homeland. But Heron's raw instinct guessed that some might return to salvage what they could, if only for pride's sake.

Having veered across the high ground to where the Scots had camped on Flodden Hill, Dacre and Heron's horsemen found stores of food and beer. Most of the camp followers had fled when they'd learned the terrible news of their army's destruction. Any who had remained in hiding were flushed out and swiftly murdered by English Borderers assigned to gather supplies and transport them back to the battlefield for the exhausted, desperately hungry and thirsty English troops. In reality, such generosity was only partly fulfilled. The Northumbrian Border men plundered and stacked much of it for themselves and were quite happy to barter or sell whatever they carried back to the field.

Against all odds, packs of Scottish resistance persisted for as long as they could see the enemy. However, a little after eight o'clock, darkness descended and the fighting dwindled, coming to a close at the mercy of the night. In the immediate aftermath, English captains and sergeants attempted to call their troops together from the free-for-all plunder of the dead, but with limited success as the men were rabid for their rightful gain. Every item, plain or precious, had its value.

Concluding the day's drama, Surrey summoned leaders from his own division together to ascertain the extent of their action. Although pale with exhaustion, the old general remained vibrant, delivering instructions heartily to his officers. The fighting had ended but not their duties. Within half an hour, fires around the field were blazing to shed light and warmth as figures roamed and mingled across the area. The thousands of long poles from the abandoned pikes scattered across the battleground provided ample wood for burning.

Meagre supplies of food and beer brought from the Flodden camp were handed to those remaining on the field until morning, but for these soldiers it meant another damp night, occupied by further torch-lit scavenging of the area, in preference to a disturbed sleep molested by nightmarish dreams of killing.

Yet, not all remained. Earlier, in dingy twilight a few regiments had set off back to Barmoor where they had camped the previous night, though taking the more direct, shorter route past Ford.

51

On Piper's Hill, Saint Cuthbert's banner, the Royal Standard and other flags had been raised. Beside a huge night fire, the weary-eyed Earl of Surrey embraced his sons and greeted his lords and knights with cautious joy. He believed in their victory but was as yet uncertain that the Scots were conquered, despite the loss of their king and a host of his leaders who had fought valiantly to the death. Darkness had fallen to terminate the conflict but Surrey was apprehensive that survivors of the Scottish army might re-form and mount another offensive come morning. Although he wished to disband his army's paid soldiers as soon as possible, relieving them of their duty and hardship – plus their expense, he needed the assurance that only tomorrow's daylight could reveal.

One by one, his commanders described the encounters they had experienced and witnessed, extolling the courage of their soldiers. It was clear that Edmund Howard's right wing had suffered most casualties and only Lord Dacre's relief had prevented annihilation. The admiral's division had coped strenuously against the three earls' assault and, backed by Sir Marmaduke Constable's Yorkshiremen plus Langley and Bulmer's Durham fighters, had whittled down the enemy, inflicting great damage. Tactically outstanding, Stanley's strategy had battered the Highlanders and wiped out the threat of their advancing to the king's rescue. Though Surrey's own division's stubborn defence had struggled to hold the king's battalions, the added support from other divisions had eventually fractured the Scots' largest force – backed by Bothwell's reserve – and inflicted dire, heavy losses including the death of their monarch.

"There is no doubt that we have had the better of it," began Surrey in his wise, unequivocal summary. "The dead do not lie," he added wryly, in support of his claim. He hesitated at the irony in his meaning, swallowed, and then continued. "England can be justly proud of what we have achieved. To you, my loyal commanders, my comrades, I offer my congratulations and my eternal gratitude. You have distinguished yourselves this day. Your boldness and diligence have inspired your soldiers. God bless them for their courage, their endurance, and their sacrifice." He concluded by asking the Bishop of Durham to lead a prayer of thanksgiving for the providence that the Almighty had bestowed upon them in their defence of England: "I implore you to praise the brave of both nations," Surrey stressed. Then, looking towards the crackling fire, his eyes widened as he summoned himself to utter words of righteousness. "For those who fight and die in battle do so valiantly," he pronounced, "and all are God's men."

Following the solemn prayers, Surrey, empowered as he was, called upon individuals to step forward to receive the honour of knighthood. It was a brief ceremony, spiritualised by the swaying gleam and shadow of firelight, peppered by light, wispy rain. Among the first of about forty to kneel on the ground before the victorious general was his younger son, Edmund, William Percy of Alnwick, John Stanley and Nicholas Appleyard.

Before Surrey and the Lord Admiral's escort left the field by torchlight, to travel through the darkness back to Barmoor Tower where they would spend the night again, they gave authority to Sir Philip Tilney for the protection of the Scottish and English artillery, and to Sir William Percy for the vigilance of the entire area. The majority of the army would remain through the night about the field, trusting that there would be no further conflict the following day, so conscripts and volunteers might begin to clear the ground of the thousands dead.

52

Towards the final hour of this tumultuous day, twelve Elsdon men sat glumly chewing morsels of food around a blazing campfire in the ruined village of Branxton. They had been given a small ration of mutton and beer from a wagon taken from the Scottish camp by Tynedale men, some of whom they knew. Although sure the Scots were well beaten, they, like the majority of fighters, were relieved, not ecstatic, at the outcome. They had risked their lives and survived but their thoughts were despondent at the death of family members and friends. Shattered by the rigours of the march and then the battle, they sat with haggard faces in melancholic silence. At their sides lay small piles of goods they had plundered from the dead.

Entering the fire's casting glow, two riders on steaming horses approached their group. They knew the tall one was called Straughen, but not the other save that he too rode with Heron. They wore helmets though each had removed his red neckerchief.

"Here," called Weatherburn heartily, swinging down from his mount and handing Little Lance a skin of beer. Straughen dismounted and both men hunkered down, joining the group around the fire.

"An' who d' we thank?" asked Lance sharply, his bald scalp glistening in the flames' light.

"Just us," stated Straughen, holding back a grin.

"Who's that'n?" Lance nodded his head at the other rider.

"My name is Adam Weatherburn," he answered happily, "famous only inside my own home."

Lance dismissed the man's humour with a frown, remaining sceptical. "What are y'u after?"

"We were told a trooper called Mossy Charlton is here. We want t' speak with 'im," said Straughen.

"It's me, here," admitted Mossy, dull-eyed in mourning of his brother's slaughter.

"Y'u found a bone-handled dagger on a dead man. We want it and will give good money for it, or something else in exchange," Straughen said bluntly.

"What if Aa want t' keep it?" griped Mossy.

Straughen eyed him coldly. "Then I'll have t' fight y'u for it."

Mossy Charlton was certainly no match for the big man. Objecting to the outlaw's audacity, Seth turned, spat on the ground and scowled at Straughen. "If it comes to fightin' one of us, you'll have t' fight us all," he threatened.

Straughen assessed the man's rugged face and the power in his broad shoulders. He grinned. "I bet y'u would. But let's tell y'u about it first. The dagger belonged to a friend of ours called Hinson who was killed yesterday, near the river, by a band of Scots. It was stolen by an English traitor named Adam Hall, and he had it on him in the fight. It was him y'u found amongst the dead. It means a lot to us that w' have it back."

"I have here somethin' y'u might like better," offered Badger Weatherburn, holding out the French count's ornate sword. He didn't need to tell them that the value of the ordinary, bone-handled dagger was nothing compared to that of the fancy sword.

Mossy's eyes gleamed. "All right then. The sword for the dagger." He picked up the dagger and was about to hand it over when Lance Milburn checked him.

"The sword first, Mossy," he advised.

"Don't say y'u don't trust us," glowered Straughen. In order to alert Weatherburn he deliberately wiped the tip of his nose. "Man, if we'd known that w' would have dealt with you differently." He gave a sharp whistle and more than twenty other men walked forward from darkness into the fire's glow and surrounded them.

Seth was infuriated. He stood up and pointed directly at Straughen. "You, big man. You against me an' no others!" he challenged, fearlessly.

Adam Weatherburn rose to his feet and beamed at Seth's bravery. "I'm delighted w' were on the same side. Not many men dare to challenge Straughen. But the's no reason t' be foolhardy. Here's the sword," he said, handing over the weapon to Mossy, who responded by giving up the dagger in exchange.

"W' thought we'd have some fun with you, that's all," admitted Straughen with a wide grin. He nodded at the newcomers and they sat down by the fire and passed round more beer and meat they'd carted from Flodden. Although Straughen gave a first impression of being slow-witted and ponderous as giant men sometimes can appear, he was acutely mindful and perceptive, as well as intrepid. He knew he had antagonised Seth and, to placate him, he went across and joined him, hunkering down. "This is a day we won't forget. A good and bad, bloody day. Good men and bad men have died. Your brother over there says you've lost two other brothers. I'm sorry to hear it."

Seth stayed silent and grim.

"Tomorrow," continued Straughen, confidentially, "we're plottin' t' find more Scots. Come with us, Seth."

Seth considered his answer before speaking. "I've had enough of killin'."

"If it was the killers of your brothers, you wouldn't say that," argued Straughen.

Seth shrugged. "Maybe not."

"Then join us."

"No."

Unhurried, Straughen stood up, hesitated, then walked away to his horse and mounted. He gave a sharp whistle and Weatherburn and the other twenty-odd swigged down their beer and left the fireside to join him, and in moments they clattered off together into the darkness.

Little Lance waited a while before he asked. "What did he say t' you, Seth?"

"He asked me t' join them. The' plan t' go after more Scots."

"What did y'u say, like?"

"Aa said 'no'."

"Good man."

53

When some of the Cheshire soldiers returned to Barmoor that night to gather their belongings, they found their baggage had been ransacked and items stolen. They were told that it was a band of Northumbrians, assigned to the right wing, which had fled the scene when the Scottish guns had first opened fire, narrowly missing them. The Cheshire men damned their very existence – a lawless northern race, notorious for their thieving, riotous and devious ways.

Recriminations against soldiers who had shown mistrust or cowardice were bitter and some acts of revenge were carried out. When a surviving group of Thomas Venables's contingent came across a bunch that had deserted them at the onset of battle, they surrounded them angrily and brayed them viciously with sticks and kicks until they yelped and pleaded for forgiveness; a forgiveness that was never given to some for the rest of their lives.

Returning to camp that same night, a dozen men from Morpeth were seized by a hot-tempered gang of Yorkshire levies who robbed them of their booty in reprisal for the thieving carried out by other Northumbrians. In retaliation, the Morpeth men, joined by more from their town, later set upon the Yorkshiremen at their campsite. To stop the brawl it took a squad of sergeants and duty soldiers with flaming torches to break them apart.

No one slept well. A drizzle of rain continued for most of the night. Everything the soldiers wore beneath their protective harness, or whatever they carried, was saturated. Though physically worn out, the brutal experiences they had endured in battle fermented images of limbless, slashed and battered bodies that rocked their minds with horror. Only the callous or disconnected managed to sleep at all.

****

It was almost midnight when Heron, dozing and wrapped in a thick cloak, woke to the sound of horses approaching. He heard Straughen's three owl whistles and emerged from the makeshift shelter on the western side of Flodden Hill, where he and two hundred riders lay in hiding. Straughen dismounted, handed his reins to Weatherburn who led the horse away, and he went to Heron. Both men sought the shelter and sat down in the timid light of a single candle. Straughen saw again the spill of dried blood showing on his leader's shirt where he had been struck on the upper left arm. Heron offered Straughen a drink of wine. The big man shook his head, preferring ale. Heron handed him the bag.

After a brief swig followed by a lick and a wipe of his mouth, a smug-faced Straughen presented the dagger. "Here it is," said Straughen enthusiastically. He told Heron how Badger had swapped it for his French sword.

Heron's eyes glimmered. "Weatherburn's a trusty man," he replied, holding up the simple-looking weapon as if it were an icon. "We've got Hinson's sword and now his dagger. If all goes right, we'll claim his silver horse tomorrow."

In the candle-lit darkness, Straughen could feel the intensity of Heron's words and saw the raven look of his face; the dark obsession that glowed out of him. Earlier, Heron had sent two informers across the Border, one into Coldstream, the other to Yetholm – to spread the news that he and his men had plundered the camp at Flodden of its riches and were settled there for the night. Confidently, Heron believed this rumour would travel fast and dearly tempt the vengeance of the Kers and other enemies dedicated to his end.

"And if they don't turn up, what will w' do then?" posed Straughen, fully aware of his leader's fanatical mind.

"We'll go after them," he replied ominously.

Straughen should have known. Drowsily, he took another gulp of beer and letting his thoughts fade, allowed himself the chance to relax before sleep eventually hauled him down.

54

During the night the rain ceased, and then the wind. Those who had managed to sleep were roused by an unusual quiet. As Saturday's dawn approached there was, for the first time in over two weeks, a pale, cloudless sky in the east, waiting for the sun to emerge and sparkle.

Heron and his men had already risen, stoked their fires and piled damp branch wood onto them to create towers of smoke. Not a voice was heard; just the odd stifled cough. The mood was sinister as about eighty of them gathered their horses and rode away, leaving the remaining hundred or so to take up their positions. In semi-darkness, Heron and his riding troop, red kerchiefs round their necks, cantered round behind Flodden's western slope to hide amongst a thicket of scrub trees and gorse bushes. Leaving Badger Weatherburn in charge, Heron and Straughen sneaked out on foot and onto a ridge above, lying down in the sodden bracken to look out across the barren upland for Scottish raiders.

Before the sun emerged, birds were already singing a tuneful welcome to a misty, bright dawn. They watched a tawny owl flapping past then heard a stream of cawing rooks and saw them whirling leisurely above the scraggy pines of a nearby rocky outcrop. Far off to their left, a small herd of roe deer raised their heads, froze identically, and then hurdled away in alarm, their white rumps bouncing. Alerted, Heron and Straughen silently focused their attention towards the moor's western edge – towards Monneylaws. Seconds later, they spied a horde of riders becoming visible on the horizon, heading towards Flodden. "Yes," breathed Heron, malevolently.

The night before, learning of the Bastard's whereabouts and the relatively few men with him, a small army of Scottish Border reivers, seeking retribution, hurriedly planned a pre-dawn raid on the camp to kill him and claim the huge ransom placed on his head by the Kers and other offended families from the Marches. This reward, and the property of the king and nobility that the English outlaws reportedly held, was a powerful draw.

Heron and Straughen ducked low as the riders came loping by, below the ridge. Among over three hundred or so Scots, they spotted the tall, bowed figure of Stoopback Ker astride Hinson's distinctive silver-haired horse. When they had passed, Heron turned his head to glance at Straughen and the redness of the dawn sky glowed in his eyes, like fever. "Come on," he rasped devilishly.

Swiftly both men scuttled back to join the others and immediately climbed onto their saddles. Turning about, the whole outfit set off at once in pursuit of the Scots who had already begun their charge into the ruined camp that they themselves had abandoned only yesterday before the battle. Smashing through the standing shelters where the smoke billowed, the Scots were dismayed to discover that no one was there.

Reining their horses around in the confusion, orders were quickly bawled – to split up into gangs and dash around the hill in search of any English; but before they were able to disperse, Heron's cavalry was heard racing towards them. At that instant, those English troopers in hiding leaped up above the bracken and triggered their deadly crossbows. Jammed in a hollow, the mounted Scots, caught between two attacks, swirled in desperation and panic. As Heron's berserk assault launched into the enemy from one side, other horsemen swept down past the bowmen into the fray, hitting them from the other.

The clash of swords and spears was furious. Men tumbled from their saddles and the wounded tried to run but there was no mercy. Confounded by the sudden ambush, many of the Scottish riders attempted to flee, including Stoopback Ker. Heron saw it and bellowed. On his horse Weatherburn instantly cut across in front of Ker and swung a mighty blow with a Highlander's sword and although Ker's shield protected him, the hefty impact unseated him. Racing across, Heron jumped down from his horse and whacked his sword's blade across Stoopback's knee before he was able to rise. The Scot squealed in pain, blood seeping through his leather boot. "No running for you," snarled Heron, turning round and continuing to fight, having ensured Ker remained on the ground, alive and captive.

Spotting Bastard Heron, the Scot, Andrew Tait, barged his horse towards him and delivered a torrent of crazed sword blows that Heron struggled to fend off with his shield, held by his weaker, injured arm. Seeing his leader's danger, Hedley from Ellingham took aim at the Scotsman's horse and shot an arrow into its flank. The horse bucked in agony and unable to hold on, the rider tumbled off. Leaping towards him, Heron needed just the one chance to drill his sword into his assailant's gut. Tait groaned and cursed before Heron struck him again in the neck.

It was only later that Heron was informed that the Scot was one of young Archie Tait's older brothers, which accounted for the frenzy of his attack.

Elsewhere, Skinner Telfer, recognising his dead brother's horse, speared the rider from behind and he dropped with the lance still sticking through him. Afterwards, retrieving his spear, the victim was seen to be Angus Ker and Skinner gloated with satisfaction, knowing he had rightly avenged his brother's slaying.

The viciousness of the ambush was overwhelming, ensuring success. Well over sixty Scots lay arrowed, gashed or maimed while the English Borderers lost no more than a dozen, though some others seemed unlikely to recover from their wounds. A number of Heron's company gave chase after the Scots that fled – but only for a short distance, enough to see the raiders gone, then they returned to the place of murder and joined the rest in their plunder of the dead. Straughen had managed to catch Hinson's horse, which had bolted, and returned with it, much to Heron's delight as he stood beside his bleeding captive. Moaning in pain on the ground, Stoopback grimaced in dread of his fate.

"Fetch a rope," ordered Heron. Weatherburn obeyed, returning quickly. "Now, tie it round his wounded leg."

Stoopback Ker groaned in agony as Weatherburn roughly looped the rope around his left ankle. Heron took hold of the rope and with Straughen's help, the three of them dragged the screaming, pleading victim over the ground to the nearest stunted oak tree and throwing the rope over the lowest branch, they rapidly heaved the rope until Stoopback was dangling upside down by his cleaved leg, his head clear of the ground. Securing the rope, they left him there writhing and went to mount their horses. Before they rode away, Heron walked his steed to the tree and tilted his head to stare pitilessly into the half-open eyes of the tortured, dying wretch.

"No more eyes for you... no more eyes," he said harshly, then cantered away towards Branxton where the drastic scene of killing was revealing itself starkly in the expanding, dazzling sunlight of a dry, bright morning.

On the forward slope of Branxton Hill where the Scottish army had formed before the battle, Heron and his soldiers paused to gaze down, observing the field of white, naked corpses among which hundreds of figures trod slowly, plundering what remained to be found. In the gleam of dawn the scale of carnage left them speechless, disbelieving of the many thousands that had been killed – all there below them, to be witnessed, as if looking down on a pale, long beach of washed-up bodies, drowned in death. Impassively, Bastard Heron sat astride his horse while, beside him, Straughen, Weatherburn, Telfer, Thompson, Hedley and the two Dunnes stared blankly, as did the rest of the cavalry in the line behind, for none had ever experienced in their lives such a vast and terrible spectacle of slaughter.

"Jesus," someone in the column muttered. And the lone word left its trail in the air.

Shouts along the hilltop turned their heads. Soldiers guarding the captured Scottish guns were warning of the return of Scottish Borderers under Home's banners. As the horsemen came into view along the west end of the ridge, Heron guessed they were almost a thousand strong, clearly hoping to retake the prized artillery of King James. Immediately, Bastard Heron raced his horsemen along the hillside towards the guns, hoping to deter the Scots for as long as possible before more riders from Dacre's cavalry could ascend the hill in support.

However, down below on Piper's Hill, the admiral, who had just arrived from Barmoor, had other plans. Alerted to the menace, he issued instructions to the English artillery, still in place, to fire uphill towards the approaching Scots. Promptly carrying out his orders, two gun blasts destroyed the calm of the valley, booming in the new day. Cannon balls thudded near the Scots, striking no one, but it was enough for many of them to take fright, turning and riding off in the direction from which they had come. Another salvo shook the air and the remainder of Home's Borderers abandoned their mission, galloping off after the others, to the relief and glee of Heron's troopers who jeered and mocked, and gestured rudely, waving their arms.

55

Since the threat had vanished, Heron and his riders now descended the hill. As his company of men retired to the ruins of Branxton village to eat and drink and recount their tales of triumph, John Heron, towing Hinson's silver mount, trotted up onto the slight ridge above the village to the spot where Surrey had directed the battle and where commanders and officers were presently waiting for the old earl's arrival from Barmoor. In the early light of morning the evidence of the slain was unmistakable; the Scottish army had been conquered and its defeat was crushing.

Amidst groups of knights conversing together, the admiral and Lord Dacre, talking with Stanley and Constable, were unaware of Heron's arrival. Then Dacre glimpsed Heron at the edge of the crowd and gladly beckoned him forward. Grateful for Heron's exploits in the battle, he greeted him with a handshake.

"Your arm, Heron, how is it?" he asked in earnest.

"It's been attended to, my Lord Dacre."

"By whom?"

"A Scottish monk."

"A Scottish monk?" repeated Dacre, puzzled.

"Indeed. One of my men found him hiding on the moor beside Flodden. Among his possessions he carried a bag of ointments and lotions. When he was brought to me I had him tend the wound and treat it accordingly."

"You hold him still, I trust?"

"Of course."

"We have many wounded in need of treatment. He can help."

"If I die he won't be helping anyone."

"What do you mean?"

"If I die, he dies too," said Heron bluntly, his sharp-featured face, curtained by his long, black hair, looked gaunt and pale with the exertion of the past days.

Lord Dacre, the esteemed Border lord, smiled wryly at a man he could admire yet still despise. Typically, Heron's caution was both wise and wicked.

"Heron," said Dacre, suddenly, his face open and sincere. "You were a lion."

Heron regarded him with bemusement as Dacre, not known to be readily cordial or to deal in praise, promptly turned about to speak to Sir William Bulmer of Durham, who waited to one side. Bulmer, known for his curtness, had once described Bastard Heron as a viper and, judging by his surly regard, he – unlike Lord Dacre – had not changed his opinion.

They did not wait long before Surrey arrived at the field. Helped down from his carriage, the old general surveyed the brutal stage whereupon the thousands of dead lay in the glistening low sunshine; their marble-white bodies, broken and shattered like fallen statues. A resigned despair misted his eyes and he felt the power of his faith clutching at his dampened heart. He raised a hand to his chest and crossed himself. Surrey squinted in sad reflection upon the abomination of murder displayed before him… the horror of it; the waste of life, and the madness of the Scottish king's folly.

After a short meeting concerning plans for the day ahead, and a delegating of duties, the Earl of Surrey turned somberly to Lord Dacre. "Find his body, my lord. You knew him better than any of us. He lies somewhere over there. I saw him." He pointed with a gnarled finger.

Dacre, Bulmer, Stanley and accompanying knights wandered off in the given direction and began searching for the monarch's dead body. They walked carefully, stepping over corpses as they stared down upon them. With the English party were two Scottish prisoners who could assist them in identifying their fallen king. On his own, John Heron was about to join the search when Surrey called for him to stay.

The old earl hobbled towards him. "Your part in this victory deserves praise," he began candidly. "We are grateful for your advice and for your courage in battle. As for myself, I am indebted to you, and to your men, for protecting my younger son Edmund, whose life was in mortal danger. It is not in my power to pardon you until that privilege is granted to me by King Henry's authority. Even now he remains in France with his army. However, I have recommended it already in my report, which is now on its way to London and Queen Catherine."

Heron looked at him squarely. "And what of my men, outlawed as well?" he asked outright.

"For their service, they too shall be acquitted of their crimes, providing they swear allegiance to the English Crown and promise to obey the laws of the land."

Heron twisted his mouth and shrugged his shoulders in mock amusement. "Here in the Borders the law of the land is to survive."

"Do you believe that they might refuse?" the earl croaked.

"Oh, no. It is an easy matter to mouth the right words. We can all say what is necessary when it's right to say it," he confessed, his expression blank.

The old earl considered the reply, and then held out his hand to shake Heron's, giving him a canny, worldly look. "Then that would be enough. We have an understanding. I shall question you no further on the matter." He grinned faintly, sympathetically, then turned and limped off to speak to his elder son, the admiral, and others awaiting him about the business of clearing the field and terminating his army's contract of service; a measure that he was keen to introduce thus relieving the Treasury's financial burden.

Heron hesitated, watching him go. Intuitively, emotionally, he knew this was a moment in his life that he would never forget: merely an old soldier limping away, small and unpretentious, but like no other. Then he too moved off, towards the group of men searching for the king's body.

The pale, white-skinned corpses lay coiled and curled and stretched in death's stiff repose. Stubbly, bearded men, shorn of their armour and clothes, bare as babes, lay woven at random across the ground in meshed patterns and piles. Though stripped of their possessions, nothing could remove the torment and anguish glued to staring eyes, open mouths, the contorted gestures of limbs and the dark, dried blood of pierced, split flesh.

The party watched glumly as common soldiers unravelled the bodies for inspection. They had identified several other nobles and gentry before discovering what they thought to be the disfigured face and body of the king. Water and a wet cloth were called for, to wipe away the clotted mess of his damaged face. As they waited, staring down at the pathetic, naked figure they presumed was James, they found themselves mute. It appeared so wrong, so unjust – the harsh aspect of his death showing him no greater or higher than any other man. Blatantly, his risk for valour had simply dishonoured him.

When the gore and grime had been carefully washed off, they recognised his short, red beard and the line of his forehead. A long, narrow scar on his right knee that he'd carried since a boyhood accident and a small mole on the curve of his neck convinced them it was, as they believed, King James's body. Lord Dacre, who knew him personally, puffed a sigh then ordered the dead king to be immediately covered and removed from the field. Raising his eyes to gaze across the scene of massacre, Thomas Dacre shook his head in distress. "May God forgive him," he uttered in true sorrow.

Grim, Stanley and Bulmer fixed their stare upon their aides, who lifted the king's corpse from the ground.

While the party trailed away following the body, borne towards Surrey who was waiting upon the small rise from which he had conducted his army in battle, only Bastard Heron remained, his eyes roaming the spot where the king had fallen. There was no purpose in his delay other than a sense of conclusion – the proof that it was done, and his revenge finally ended. About to turn away he glimpsed a minute, blue sparkle in the mud – a piece of stone or metal glinting in the angled, early morning sun. Idly, he used the toe of his boot to uncover it and his curiosity made him bend down. Extracting the object from the soil with his gloved hand, he rubbed away the dirt and examined his find. A faint shudder crossed his heart. He tensed, his lips parting. He stood up, bewildered. He was not mistaken. It was her brooch; a token he, James, had carried to his death.

Heron's despair gave way to bitterness. The king had loved her. The thought resounded in his mind. He strode off the field, mounted his horse and fled, as he always did, from the anguish of injured feelings.

56

The huge operation of clearing the ground had been organised by officers under the direction of Sir William Percy. Beneath a beaming sun, the morning's task of digging was well under way when Surrey, observing the huge undertaking, turned to Sir Marmaduke Constable. "I wish to discover the fate of a soldier from the East Riding Company, and whether he survived the battle. His name is Snitch, Edward Snitch, from the Sculcoates area."

The small, rotund Yorkshire nobleman nodded. "I shall ask one of my aides to attend to it. And if he lives, do you wish to speak with him?" he added, wrinkling his brow.

"Perhaps. But if he indeed lives, I rightly desire him to know that he has performed his duty as an Englishman." The earl cleared his throat, after which his expression seemed to soften. "I also wish for you to accompany me to the church, where our own knights are to be laid alongside King James. I am weary, Constable, and need you, my friend, at my side," he requested.

Sir Marmaduke bowed slightly towards his Commander-in-Chief, his comrade and confidant. "Fortune has proven you to be a great general. History will not, however, tell of the unique man that I – and others who have served under you – know, admire and respect," he averred benignly.

Surrey smiled faintly. "Fortune indeed!" he affirmed. "Had the king brought his army down to fight us on the plain at Milfield, as we first desired, it would probably be him now breathing in this day's air, not you and I. Or, indeed, had we managed to ascend Branxton Hill as planned and engaged the Scots on the moor, I doubt we would have overcome them as we did on this field here. But..." He bowed his head in return for Constable's praise. "But I thank you, my noble friend for your loyal esteem."

Surrey paused, considering what else he should add. "Yes, history will tell what it can. It will speak of the victory and the loss. It will recall the events before, during and after the battle. It may note the misery, the hunger, the desperation and the fear of soldiers. It will describe the valour and courage of men from both sides and how fate turned triumph our way. Yet it cannot show the true pain: the hurt, the sorrow, the woe and grief, nor the individual acts of heroism and wickedness; the thrill and terror; the relief and remorse in the hearts of those who fought, lived or died. That is not a story for history; sentiment counts for little in the facts that history shall record and present for later generations. Oh yes, we are victorious. And we are rightly proud of it. Yet you, Sir Marmaduke, and I both know from our experience of war that in the eyes of God, only man's evil is the ultimate victor in the killing of one another."

In dignified silence, the two ageing noblemen gazed compassionately across the field of dead soldiers; a tragic, gruesome picture of human disaster – the summation of a king's failure and an old earl's crowning achievement.

57

In gleaming morning sunshine, the Elsdon men searched for their own dead over the stretch of land where Edmund Howard's division on the right had been critically overcome. It was here that English casualties were higher than elsewhere, due to the success of the long pikes' charge over flatter, firmer ground.

They were not the only ones embarked upon such a task. Groups of men from Lancashire and Cheshire were also weeding their way through areas of dead where their own had suffered terrible loss. It was reckoned that almost the entire Macclesfield unit had perished with their leader, Sir Christopher Savage. Surrey had earlier instructed that the bodies of the nobility and gentry, including Savage, Thomas Venables and Robert Fouleshurst be carried to the village church to receive blessings and preparation for transportation home to their estates. This was not to be the case for ordinary soldiers. Unless carted away by family or friends, they were destined to be buried in mass graves. Supervised by sergeants, the digging of these pits was well under way, employing soldiers and some local folk eager for payment. These locals readily admitted that yesterday afternoon from a nearby hill, a crowd of them, spectators, twisted by curiosity, had safely viewed the battle.

Seth Milburn, his brother Dick and their uncle, Little Lance, along with Mossy Charlton, knew where to find their dead, having fought alongside them. In the storm of battle there had been no time to reflect upon their fall, but now, combing through the debris of corpses, the four of them grieved their loss and shed tears when they found them in the mud, battered and stripped. Upon seeing the state of their bodies, they were all the more determined to take them home for burial, where they were known and where their families could mourn and honour them, and visit their graves.

News of the battle's outcome had by now, late morning, reached the site at Wooler. Here, the camp followers had stayed to clear the ground and wait in hope for their men and relatives to return, and gather up what they had left behind before venturing home. Mossy and Dick agreed to set off at once to Wooler and return to Branxton with ponies and cart, thereby enabling them to transport their dead, home to Redesdale. To console himself, Mossy was desperate to see Jenny, his wife, and for her to know that he was safe, and to hold her in his arms again.

Once they had left, Seth and Lance and others worked together to lift and carry their family dead from the field, down to the village, laying the bodies side by side. Close by, two cousins from Otterburn guarded a stack of possessions and bounty. About the village were hundreds of other groups of men, and any loot left unsupervised was ripe for thieving.

Later, for some peculiar, unknown reason, Seth felt the need to return to the scene of slaughter. This time he went alone and wandered again through the swathes of dead, towards a bunch of men dragging bodies to the edge of the first pit that would soon be deep enough for the corpses to be thrown in. He was not attracted to the grisly business but by an instinct that compelled him to go there, bound by expectation. Presently, he came across two figures wrestled together, a Scot and an English soldier, who had perhaps struck each other simultaneously, fallen, strained to rise then slumped to the ground, locked together in death. Seth's heart thudded with pity. He shook his head in dismay and turning away from the pair, he suddenly spotted the prone body of the young Scottish lad he had spared in the turmoil of violence that had engulfed them.

He knelt down beside him. The boy seemed as though he were sleeping, lying on his front, head turned sideways. His face looked peaceful and innocent. Seth knelt down and turned him over and saw the dark, red hole in his chest. Seth sighed as he reflected on the mercy that had been shared yet spared only him. Picking up the dead, naked boy, he cradled him from the field and laid him down.

Venturing across to a pit where men were digging, he helped himself to a metal pick and wooden shovel. An angry officer challenged him but Seth marched past him and the man sensed with good reason that he dare not obstruct him. Seth strode back to the dead boy and began to dig a shallow trench in which to lay him. Afterwards, covering the small grave with rocks and stones to prevent wild creatures clawing it open, Seth stood in silence, unable to find words to say anything of how he felt. Turning, he trudged off, weaving his way through the rubble of butchered dead and the sombre groups at work, clearing the field.

Attracted by the scent of blood, the sky above swarmed with carrion crows greedily stalking the scene; some already strutted the ground, heads turning, wary of movement.

58

They strode between four guards at the porch entrance and, stepping past the heavy wooden door and out of the bright midday sun, the admiral and John Heron blinked, adjusting their eyes to the dim, candle-lit interior of the church. Laid out on pallets, and wrapped in cloaks and blankets, thirteen dead English nobles reposed on the floor. At the chancel archway, upon a raised trestle, the corpse of King James was fully covered-over by a torn banner.

A priest wearing a black cassock bowed towards them, and then made his exit.

Admiral Howard, with Heron following him, walked down the short nave, passing by the king's body, and knelt before the altar. Each man crossed himself and then Howard recited a short psalm. Heron joined him with an "Amen." Rising, the two men crossed themselves once more and turned to leave. They were bound by silence. The obligation between them was now closed and the admiral was satisfied.

Outside, in brightness, they mounted their horses. The admiral peered up at the cloudless, blue sky. "Today the sun shines for us. Yesterday it was God. Remember that," he insisted with gravity in his voice and face. "My father believed in you from the start, Heron. Do not forget that, either," he added before spurring his horse, to leave, alone.

Solemn, Bastard Heron stared after him until he disappeared over the facing ridge. Then he climbed down from his horse once more and re-entered the church. The guards grew tense as he passed.

Unaccompanied, he stepped down the aisle again and, stopping where King James lay, he turned back the covering and stared at the wrapped face hiding the ghastly wounds. Heron's shadow fell across it. "You loved her too, didn't you?" he mumbled. "What fools we've been." He paused, put back the cover and wandered over to a recess and, in the dimness, sat on a small ledge. With a ponderous stare he waited, and his thoughts replayed the events of the previous day: the long march; his duel; the battle; his wound; how Edmund survived and the victory unfolded in the failing light with the gallant Scots inexorably falling, dying for a king that had led them to needless ruination.

He thought of Hinson and Telfer, ambushed by the river. He thought of other men lost to him, such as the Dunne twins, and of those, like himself, fortunate to have survived. And he considered his revenge, regaining Hinson's sword, dagger and horse. And he knew it was not over; that there would never be peace inside him. His care was wrapped in a cold heart of hatred and unforgiving. Violence was his shield and flight his armour. Without them he was weak, vulnerable to the stabbings of rejection and loneliness.

Perhaps an hour had passed when he heard the church door open and his reverie was immediately extinguished, like a candle's flame. Footsteps approached, soft and slow. Lady Heron appeared, escorted by her two maids. All three were veiled against the smell of death. Standing beside the king's shroud, Lady Elizabeth discerned his figure concealed in the corner. She asked her escorts to leave her and that they wait outside. When they had done so, John Heron stood up and approached her from the dimness. They stood facing each other as the king's body lay at rest between them.

She raised her veil. "How long have you been waiting for me?" she asked, pathos in her weary eyes.

He shrugged. "A little while. Not long."

She did not respond, but gazed at him sorrowfully.

"I wish to show you this." He held up the brooch. She showed no reaction. "The king carried it into battle with him. I found it in the mud." His voice sounded hollow and emotionless. He held it out for her and she took it in her hand and gazed down at it. Her eyes flickered.

"I loved him," she admitted in a whisper, clenching the brooch in her hand. "I loved him as I once loved you, and as I love my husband, William. I can't explain," she confessed. Riven with emotion, her voice was frail.

Bastard Heron turned his regard from her, his eyes staring numbly at the wall, their glint – dark and bleak. She noticed the bandage around his arm.

"You are wounded," she remarked.

He looked longingly at her. "As I have been, always, and for the rest of my days."

She shook her head slowly. "Oh, John," she sighed. "Your life is but a shadow – its careless soul enraging your inner self, like poison. Why do you persecute yourself so, my dear, poor John?"

"If pity is all you can offer me, I'll keep the brooch instead," he answered acridly, extending his hand. A glimmer of ire and denial embittered his face.

Her eyes widened in dismay. Disturbed by his wild, estranged look, she gently placed the brooch into his palm.

He straightened himself, his expression severe and harrowed. The torment of Heron's misery swirled from his gut to every edge of himself. In the cool stillness within the church he sensed the presence of God there for him. He shied away from it. "Goodbye, my lady," he ended hoarsely, condemning himself to a moment's gaze, beholding her beauty and its aura for the last time, before pivoting round and leaving her there, alone with him, the king of her affections.

In the bright, warm sunshine, John Bastard Heron lurched past the silent guards and tremulous maids, who stepped back from his path. Grabbing the reins of his horse, he swung up and galloped away to join his men at their encampment.

From his vantage point on Piper's Mount, Surrey spotted the red cape and watched his flight, racing uphill towards Flodden. Sensing he was gone and would not return, that they may likely never meet again, old Surrey drew his sword and raised it above his head in a final, parting gesture of farewell.

59

The dead were heaped into the pits. For every English corpse – Edward Snitch was not one – there were at least four Scots. Enemies in life, united in death, they lay together undivided, their pale, cold, feeble-looking bodies, naked and silent. Once buried, they were hidden forever, lost to everything that was meaningful in life, and to everyone that knew them; save in memory.

****

Scotland wailed and shuddered at its tragedy and the catastrophe of its failure. Not a single community was untouched, and every family suffered the death of a husband, father, son, brother or some other relation. In a number of cases there was complete loss, as with Jock Burn and his three sons who fought and died in the battle.

Those that survived returned as gaunt figures, a dull feature of their former selves. They walked back into a world that remained theirs but in which they felt removed, as if strangers. The wounded clung to their existence but many, infected, were unable to recover, and perished. At night, asleep, men would often jolt awake in sweat, minds and conscience ravaged by memories of screaming soldiers, of flesh and bone wrenched and shredded open by a hail of blows.

The depleted nation prepared itself for an English invasion that was not forthcoming and its hastily appointed leaders rued the ill suffered by their country, which King James's stubborn aspiration had inflicted upon them. To ensure stability, Queen Margaret's son was quickly crowned King James V. Alas, he was only seventeen months old. On his behalf, the Duke of Albany returned from France and was appointed Governor of Scotland. This did not, however, salve the bitter, old rivalries between powerful factions that schemed against each other to gain greater authority; their enmity resulting in strife and intrigue at all levels. The security and importance of Scotland that King James IV had established was swiftly undone. And before long, attracted by diplomacy, France and England aimed to befriend each other in a new treaty. Thus, Scotland, like its dead king, found itself relegated in the eyes of Europe and its authority and influence in decline.

After his death, James IV's body was embalmed at Berwick and then the corpse was transported south to London. Although the Earl of Surrey wished for him to be commemorated in some way, this seemed to be passed over by King Henry and his advisors, and soon ignored. At Sheen Priory, the body was stored, left, ignominiously moved, removed and over time gradually forgotten until its remains were buried, much later, at an unmarked site – the once esteemed, lauded Scottish king, now eternally invisible.

The Earl of Surrey, for his service to king and country, was restored to his Dukedom of Norfolk – his son, the admiral, inheriting the title Earl of Surrey. Though credit was given to the leader and his noble commanders for their victorious campaign, repelling the great Scottish army, there was no national celebration. Nevertheless, it was widely admired across the realm. However, Henry's expensive invasion of France had gained only moderate success and since the triumph of Flodden was not his, it was easily, if not deliberately, underplayed.

The aged English commander, Thomas Howard, second Duke of Norfolk, lived for another ten years after the battle and died peacefully at home in May 1524, aged eighty, his adoring wife at his bedside. His funeral was immense, befitting a triumphant soldier – a bold and gracious man.

His son, the earl – and still the Lord Admiral, continued to rise in stature and in politics, becoming a prominent figure in the Tudor Court and a close adviser to King Henry VIII. As was the fickle nature of politics at that time, he too fell out of favour, was imprisoned, as his father had once been, released and then reinstated to become the third Duke of Norfolk.

Sir Edmund Howard followed a far less distinguished path than his older brother, achieving only the minor position of Controller of Calais, from which he was eventually dismissed. A year after that, he also died, in 1539.

Seth and Dick Milburn took their brothers home for burial. Mossy Charlton gave Davie a proper funeral at Hepple, near Elsdon. Little Lance carted Harry Milburn back to Otterburn to allow his sister to see him buried there. Willie and John Dunne took the twins' bodies back to Kyloe. The bodies of Hinson and Joe Telfer were dug up on the moor where they had been quickly buried and transported down to the church graveyard at Doddington. They were the fortunate ones to avoid the pits and the anonymity of being dumped there. Only fortunate, that is, in the treatment of the dead.

The Scots' crushing defeat resulted in well over ten thousand of them being flung into the mass graves, most of them anonymous, unknown soldiers. Peasants, labourers, craftsmen, gentlemen, knights and nobility, heaped together without ceremony, without the dignity and blessing they deserved.

However, the names of the dead Scottish commanders and officers were recorded. Well over a hundred of them, the cream of a nation, rash and bold in their devotion and loyalty to a beloved, inspirational, but misguided king.

A threat to Albany, Alexander, Lord Home was arrested for treason. As commander of the Scottish left-wing division at the battle, he had ordered his exhausted soldiers from the field after their initial success against Edmund Howard's division. A return to the fray by Huntly and his Gordon clansmen, and the brave earl's death, sealed Home's conviction; found guilty, he was executed in 1516.

Bastard Heron gained his royal pardon. In reality this meant he now only needed to look over one shoulder, not both. He and his troopers continued their raiding and reprisals against the Scots. For a while after the battle his name flourished on the Border, but he proved to be an unsatisfactory hero. The grisly ordeal of Flodden made him more callous. He became increasingly petulant and violent, more desperate and unscrupulous, hell-bent on danger and destruction.

One moonlit night in June 1524, a month after the Duke of Norfolk's death, the Kers and their allies encircled Heron's raiding party and slashed their way towards him. Thanks to Straughen's courage and sacrifice, Bastard Heron managed to escape though his wounds were serious. Two nights later, on his bed at Crawley Tower, alone, without company or love, he died, aged thirty-nine – a year younger than King James when killed at the Battle of Branxton, better known as Flodden.

Beneath Heron's pillow lay an opal brooch.

60

A year later, on a sunny June morning, in a small meadow near his cottage outside Elsdon, Seth Milburn was scything grass to make hay. Nearby, his two young sons stood ready with strong sticks to club any rabbits that might spring from the long grass. Their attention was turned by the sound of horses. They stopped to watch a band of horsemen driving cattle across the stream below, following a track through the pasture. The helmeted riders were reiver men, returning from a night's raid into Scotland. They were close enough for Seth to see them clearly and he knew that they were not local men. In itself that was not surprising for raiders often strayed far along the Border in search of quarry.

One of the leading riders waved the others on and detached himself from them, pausing to stare towards Seth and his boys. Seth tensed, gripping his fork tighter and ordered the boys to run to the house while he remained. The rider walked his horse forward and halted a few steps away, studying Seth's face and his broad frame.

"Is your name Seth Milburn?" he asked.

Seth didn't recognise the voice. "It might be," he replied, his rough face set stern.

The horseman removed his helmet and shook his hair free. Seth saw the red kerchief round his neck and the white streak along the top of the thick brown hair. Seth eased, relaxing his stance. He nodded in remembrance, and then smiled a greeting.

Weatherburn climbed down and warmly shook Seth's hand. "Aa thought it was you – the man who challenged the mighty Straughen." He grinned.

"Aa heard about him bein' killed. And Heron dyin' of his wounds. Aa was sorry t' hear of it," said Seth.

Weatherburn paused in reflection. "There was about five hundred o' them. We fought them as hard as w' could but the' was too many. Aa was lucky to get away."

"And you're still at it, eh?"

Adam Weatherburn gave a wry smile. "We're still Heron's men. It's in the blood."

Seth chuckled. "Aa've never fought a man since the battle. It was enough for me an' those of us here that came back alive."

"Aa wish I had your good sense. It's not often Aa meet a man I admire more than m'self," he declared humorously.

Amused, Seth's face beamed as it could with full force. They talked a little while longer, Seth telling the other how he'd married and the boys were his – another good reason to live out of danger's way.

Weatherburn agreed, then putting his helmet back on, he mounted and turned his horse. "Has Mossy still got the fancy sword?" he asked, swivelling round in the saddle.

"Aye, he has." Seth sounded as if he were there again, round the fire, reliving the time.

"And what about the bald man with y'u that didn't trust us?" asked Weatherburn.

"That was Lance from Rothbury," Seth grinned. "Aye, he's still goin' about. When w' came back from Branxton Moor he found himsel' a wife from Otterburn. A sister t' one of ours that got killed."

"Well Aa never," exclaimed Badger Weatherburn. He pulled out his bone-handled dagger. "An' A've still got Hinson's knife." He gave a wild laugh and rode off to catch up with the others; still Heron's men.